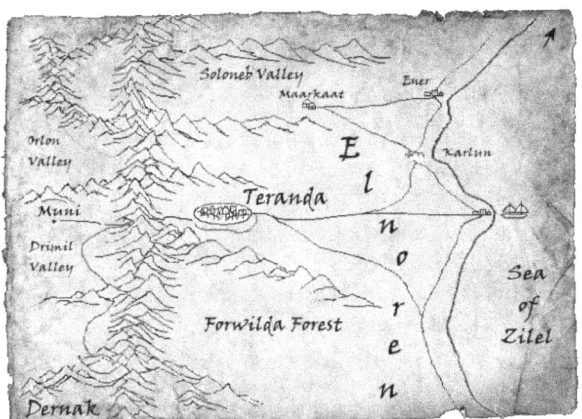

The region of Elnoren

CONTENTS

I dedicate this book to my
family, friends
and to God
for the grand adventure

Swords of Men and Angels

THE
AWAKENED
CITY

In the early days of Earth's history, humanity grew in numbers and quickly spread across the lands subduing everything before them even the great dinosaurs.

With increasing imagination of the arts and the shaping of stone, they built great cities of magnificent splendor. They mastered the forging of steel and the making of great weapons of war.

They gathered into armies and conquered with war. Slowly they forgot their maker as their pride led to evil desires.

As the sons of Cain increased in wickedness, the sons of Seth stood against them with great faith in their Creator. Stories turned to legend as one sword rose to infamy. Said to be forged by the hand of God, many believed it gave the wielder great victories and much more.

Chapter 1
THE FALLEN KING

The water sparkled in the sun's rays as it flowed down the narrow river. In the clear blue water, fish swam gently going up and down the current while remaining close to each other.

Suddenly an arrow whistled through the air, and pierced the undisturbed water. A thin line attached to the arrow followed behind. After a brief moment, the line went taut and a young man standing on a small cliff beside the river began to haul upward. His horse, tied to a tree several paces away, watched him calmly.

As the arrow came out of the water, a fish dangled at its point. Slowly, the young man happily brought the line in and grabbed the fish with a satisfied smile.

His name was Dunen, second son to Favro, king of Teranda. His face was soft but with firm features; his eyes were black and curious, and his hair was dark brown. He was of medium height compared to most men of the region, but sure-footed, strong and walked confidently as one would raised up in a great and proud family.

Occasionally, Dunen left the palace and city life to

spend some peaceful moments beside the river that came from the mountains.

He loved to fish and practice archery in his private spot. Sometimes using fish as targets, he believed, offered a greater challenge than the fixed targets used in training. Moving targets were harder to hit, helping him to acquire a better sense of direction to his aim.

As he sat down to remove the fish from the shaft of his arrow, the sound of a horse's hooves in the woods attracted his attention. Dunen raised himself to see who came. Through a narrow path in the forest, he watched as a horse and rider approached.

"Dunen!" a girl's voice cried out.

Dunen immediately recognised Aristinne's voice. She was the daughter of a landlord in Teranda. Her family were close friends of his, and some even wondered if they would one day marry. Although Dunen liked Aristinne's companionship, his interest never grew more than a friendship.

"Here I am," he shouted back as she came to the small clearing.

Dressed in her beige leather riding clothes, she dismounted her mare. As she approached Dunen, she gave him the customary bow of respect. Dunen found this annoying since he considered her a close friend and moreover reminding him of his princely position.

"I was sent to fetch you," she said happily.

"By whom?" he asked as he returned to removing the arrow from the fish.

"Master Penahas. He said your father wants your presence at the hall," she informed him as she watched him with interest.

"Trouble again, I presume," he said annoyingly as he wrenched the fish from his arrow. "My father wants me to learn how he deals with the landlords of the city."

"He does well. You are a prince and heir to the throne," Aristinne said, secretly hoping that someday he would become king.

"I do not want to become king. My father has chosen Tharan. He is the firstborn and the right choice. My brother will be an excellent king, and I will stand by his side," Dunen said proudly.

Aristinne smiled, admiring his devotion and humble spirit.

"Let us go," he said as he cast the fish aside and picked up his bow and arrows.

Dunen helped Aristinne to mount her horse and then untied his and mounted. They were soon off, cantering headlong through the woods, the sun peaking in and out from behind the trees as they rode.

Teranda lay on a large plateau, in the midst of a valley and surrounded by forests. Not far to the west, the great Magdin Mountains crossed from north to south. Apart from the inner valley and the mountain pass of Perethes, any other way to the city was perilous and very difficult.

Teranda's great stone walls protected the city with their height and thickness. Only a few homes and the royal palace rose above the high walls and could be seen only from a distance. From the day they were made by king Anandun, Dunen's grandfather, no army was able to overcome them. Throughout the lands, the walls of Teranda were well known and respected.

Dunen and Aristinne approached Teranda from the north, galloping toward the main gates. A flow of merchants and peasants entered and exited through the gates of the city, while the city guards cautiously watched them pass.

As Dunen joined the flow, the people waved and saluted their young prince and the guards bowed.

Teranda's streets were filled with people going

about their business as Dunen and Aristinne trotted up the main road.

"I beg your leave, Dunen," Aristinne said unwillingly as they came to a cross street that led to her own house. "My mother awaits me."

"Farewell, Aristinne. Salute your parents for me. Tell them I will come to visit them soon," Dunen promised as he watched her go.

She waved and was glad to hear of his promise.

Dunen arrived at the palace square and found it busy as usual. Servants and personal guards of visiting landlords moved around as they waited for their masters' business to end with the king or with the officials of the city. The palace servants scurried as they attended to their needs during their stay.

The royal palace rose several stories high, its ivory walls glistening in the sun. Great towers rose even higher, topped with flags bearing the royal family's emblem of a golden lion. Great white arches and pillars decorated the walls. White marble steps led to the huge main doors. A small stone wall surrounded the palace, and a large arched entrance opened the way. The entrance had no gates or doors.

As Dunen came to the palace steps, servants came immediately to take care of his horse the moment he dismounted.

As he walked up the stairs, Penahas appeared at the guarded doors. Penahas was Dunen's family advisor. He was a thin and fragile man and yet he seemed never tired of all the duties given to him by the King. He was well loved and honoured for his wisdom and loyalty.

"Dunen!" he said, giving a quick bow. "Your father wishes you by his side in complete uniform."

"I heard, Penahas. Who has come to the throne?" Dunen asked as they began to enter the palace together.

"Lurion," Penahas answered ominously.

Dunen gave him a look of disgust, "He comes to challenge my father again. He is bold."

"Not by his own strength, I can assure you. He is under great suspicion," Penahas added.

"If you believe the rumours that he serves Ernum. I doubt it not, Penahas," Dunen returned with a smirk.

Penahas smiled and was glad the young prince was informed of the current affairs of the throne.

The two walked through the wide corridor. Stone arches curved above them with delicate design and the marble floor shone with many intricate patterns.

"We know nothing yet of his dealings," Penahas wondered.

"I am sure my father knows more than we what goes on with this snake. He will know how to deal with him," Dunen said confidently.

They both left the corridor and turned to take the stairs that led to the family quarters.

"I go to your father. Be quick, or he will be displeased with me," Penahas begged.

"Fret not, I will," Dunen assured him as he stepped up the winding stairs.

Dunen reached his room and found servants waiting to dress him. Large windows with a view of the northern mountains were opened, allowing a small breeze to come through, swaying the burgundy drapes. A door beside the windows led to a small balcony. In the large chamber, Dunen's bed was against one wall, covered with a light blue quilt. Another wall held banners and trophies won by him in festivals, competitions, and in his various studies.

Dunen removed his riding clothes, and the servants immediately helped him with his armor.

"Will you be wearing your helmet, my lord?" a servant asked.

"No. My sword only," he answered, and a servant brought his sword and scabbard and tied it to his waist.

Dunen wondered if his presence at the hall was of any real use. He had seen enough of these confrontations to last him a lifetime.

Suddenly, sounds of men shouting could be heard outside. At first, Dunen and his servants looked at each other and wondered the reason for the upheaval and then they heard the trumpets. Dunen's heart skipped as he recognized the warning of an attack on the city.

Dunen and his servants rushed to the balcony and looked down into the palace courtyard. The servants gasped with astonishment at what they saw.

Below, Dunen could see to his surprise, his royal guard fighting armed peasants. As he watched the struggle, he was even more astonished to see his soldiers losing the fight. Shocked with unbelief, he took a closer look at the peasants and discovered their swordsmanship revealed them as enemy soldiers in disguise. Instantly, Dunen realised that this was a secret attack, and a very dangerous situation.

In all the frenzy, Dunen saw many more armed peasants rush toward the palace. Guessing they would soon be outnumbered, Dunen thought of his family.

Fearful, he ran out of his room, leaving the troubled servants behind. Just as he ran toward the stairs, he heard the clatter of swords and the shouting of men. In the stairs, two of his soldiers were keeping back three or more assailants. The way blocked, Dunen decided to get to the throne hall by way of the hall balconies. Racing down the long corridor, he came to the door that led to the balconies that overlooked the throne hall. Opening the door, he rushed in and halted abruptly at the scene below. The throne hall was in a tumult of fighting and clanging steel. On the throne dais, Dunen saw his father and brother fighting off several opponents. Only half a dozen or so palace guards were banded together near the king while the rest were scattered.

Although his people fought well, the enemy soldiers kept coming. Dunen feared for his father and wanted to be by his side.

The door to the gallery burst open and two invaders with raised swords in hand came running toward Dunen.

Dunen swiftly drew his sword and took them on. With deftness he kept them off until he found an opening and stabbed one opponent. Without any hesitation, Dunen dealt with the remaining one as the other crumbled to the floor. With great anger, Dunen dispatched his enemy and turned back at the scene below.

His father's band of guards had diminished and as he watched with fear, he could see his father looking around the room, searching anxiously for someone, while keeping his opponents away. Dunen realised his father was looking for him.

"Father!" he shouted over the noise.

As he shouted again, his father looked up and spotted him. For a moment, as they looked at each other, Dunen saw sadness in his father's face. King Favro then did the unexpected. He first stuck hard his opponents away giving him space to take his sword and with one great swing, throw it toward Dunen. Dunen watched it spin through the air and slammed against the stone wall of the balcony falling on the floor only a few feet away.

As Dunen turned back to look at his father, his heart stopped. Unarmed, the attackers stabbed the King. Pierced by two swords, the King fell backward to the floor. With shock and disbelief, he watched his horrified brother try to reach his father only to be struck down also.

"No!" Dunen screamed in great agony as he felt his world fall below him.

Weakened by the horror, Dunen fell to his knees in tears. Shocked at the thought of his father and brother's deaths, he remained stunned with disbelief and could hardly breathe.

Looking away from the scene below, his eyes fell on his father's sword and, at that moment, his years of training came to him. His father had passed the sword to him and it was now his duty to keep it safe. From his childhood, he was trained and told that such an event could happen, and yet he could never believe it. He remember that his duty was to take the sword and escape, but at that moment Dunen's anger demanded revenge for his father and brother's death even though he knew what his father would want him to do.

The sound of running steps drew his attention as other enemy soldiers came running toward him from the living quarters.

Watching them come, he could hear his father say: "We live for God, and so we also fight for Him when He chooses the time."

The words instantly brought his training into action. He knew that he must survive this horrific moment, not only for himself but for his family and the people of Teranda.

Raising his eyes above, he prayed. "My God! Stand with me now!" he cried, and then quickly tossing his sword aside, he picked up his father's sword.

With a burning anger that grew by the second, Dunen rose to meet his enemies and struck his enemies with a blind frenzy. In a short moment, one was dead, and the second fearfully backed away and ran the way he came. Dunen stood there panting, his blood racing through his veins and some running down his wounded arm and from smaller cuts. As he watched the soldier run off, he realised he had to do the same and escape.

The enemy had taken the palace and probably the city. He was now the only living heir to the throne, and they would want him dead. He must flee before he was found, he thought. He must live to avenge his father and brother's death which now fuelled his burning goal.

Looking one last time at the throne, Dunen saw the cloaked figure of Rondree staring up at him. He was Lurion's military advisor, and Dunen was sure that the attack was all his doing. Immediately

Dunen raced off into the palace. As he ran, the horrid scene replayed in his mind, but Dunen forced himself to turn the thoughts away.

"Lord God, protect me," he prayed. "Show mercy on my father's house."

At that moment, he remembered his mother. Coming to an abrupt halt in a corridor, he wondered where she was. He had completely forgotten her. Dunen considered returning into the palace to look for her, but the sounds of fighting warned against it. With much sorrow, he continued his way to the rear of the palace while suppressing the guilt of his decision.

Descending a flight of stairs, he came on a surprised enemy soldier and slew him before he could defend himself. On he ran through the corridors, his heart pounding with fear and pain.

Exiting through a door at the rear of the palace, Dunen saw several of his guards fighting the enemy. The palace stalls were a hundred paces away.

One soldier on seeing his lord sprinted to his side.

"My lord! Lurion has done this," he shouted with anger.

Dunen's whole being begged for his death.

"What is my lord's command?" the soldier asked,

gathering his breath from his struggles.

How could Lurion have dared such a plan, Dunen thought? Ernum was the only answer that came to his mind.

"Come, we must escape. The city is taken," Dunen said as he ran to the horses.

"What of my king and lord Tharan?" the soldier asked as he followed.

"Dead!" Dunen could hardly say to the shocked soldier as he held back the pain from surfacing.

Quickly they untied two horses and led them out. As soon as they mounted, they kicked their horses to a gallop. Before they could get away from the palace, three assailants attacked them. Dunen deflected a thrust to his chest and kicked the soldier away. Another replaced him, and Dunen parried his swing and then cut him through the neck. Looking around, he saw the palace courtyard filled with dead and fighting men. His soldier had killed his opponent and was ready to follow him.

Dunen turned away from the ghastly scene, and rode his horse toward the streets of the city. As they galloped through the streets, people jumped out of the way in fear as women watched from their windows with horror and dread, many of which were crying, Dunen wanting to join them.

"Horsemen!" the soldier shouted to Dunen.

Dunen looked back and saw half a dozen men coming after them. He hoped that the gates were not taken, or else he would have to use another way out of the city. Through the winding cobblestone roads they clattered, with their foes not far behind. All of a sudden, Dunen heard his soldier cry out. Looking back, he saw his soldier fall off his horse with an arrow in his back. His sadness deepened as he thought of all the loyal men who died to defend his family and city. The fear for his life worsened and yet he controlled himself not wanting to fail his father. Not a second passed before an arrow deflected against the side of his armor. Dunen began to veer his horse from side to side, making it difficult for the archer to hit him. Several misses soon after proved his manoeuvre worked.

Arriving at the wall, he followed it toward the gates. To his great relief, the doors were opened, but a great battle raged around them. Dunen carefully entered the fray and engaged in several combats as he moved toward the doors. As he cut down an opponent, he felt an arrow strike his side and pierce through his coat of mail and pierce him. With great pain Dunen grabbed the arrow and broke it off. Putting aside his injury, he clenched his teeth and moved on toward freedom. Slashing away those who dared to bar his way, he finally broke through and galloped off toward the forest. Behind him, the clamour of steel striking steel and the cries of men faded as the calm world of the forest welcomed him in.

Chapter 2
SAFE HAVEN

Injured and feeble, Dunen rode his horse slowly and aimlessly through the woods. It was late afternoon, two days after Lurion had taken Teranda. The light of day began to disappear within the dense forest. Besides the rustling of the trees moved by a light breeze, only the horse's heavy steps could be heard in the darkening woods. Dunen sat slumped forward on the saddle and swayed at every movement. Trails of dried blood came down from cuts in his arms and large patches of blood smeared his armor. His sheathed sword dangled to one side.

Abruptly, the horse neighed with a low cry of exhaustion and halted. Dunen lazily raised himself to see what had disturbed his horse. Weariness and sadness hung heavy on his face mixed with sweat and long streaks of tears through the grim. Looking ahead into the dim forest, his eyes perceived a glimmer of light. At first he thought it was a dream until he caught the smell of fire. He's curiosity turned to fear then anger at the thought of an enemy camp for he was sure they searched for him.

He stiffened his posture with defiance and instinctively reached for his sword. But after a moment of consideration, Dunen relaxed and returned to his feeble position, realizing this campfire was too small for soldiers of the city. Kicking his horse weakly, he urged it forward.

In a clearing, not far away, a small fire gave light against the darkness that surrounded it. Close by the fire, a tall and huge bronze-skinned man searched vigorously in his saddle bag. With a huge grin, he ended his search and pulled out a leather pouch. As he moved towards the fire, he eagerly opened the pouch and despite his size, sat crossed-legged with ease. A large sword, scarred by much use, lay by his side. Its worn grey metal reflected the fire's light. The frame of the man was muscular and firm. His hands were large, with thick fingers. The man's clothes bulged and shifted at his every move. His face was round and jolly and his windblown hair was dark brown like the earth.

Out of the leather bag, he retrieved a big piece of cheese and relished the thought of eating it, his eyes gleaming with hunger. As he licked his lips, he quickly reached near his waist for a small dagger and began to cut a large piece of the cheese.

Before he could take a bite, the rustling of the bushes attracted his attention. In a heartbeat, although his great size, he was on his feet and ready to fight. His large sword no longer lay idle on the ground, but was in his hand, stretched out forward menacingly.

Not far from the clearing, Dunen appeared, halting his horse just at its border. The light of the fire barely revealed him in the flickering shadows.

The villager recognised the armor of a city dweller, and was a bit surprised to find him in these northern parts and so late in the day.

"May I share the warmth of your fire?" Dunen asked slowly and with some difficulty.

With hesitation and suspicion the villager answered. "If you are a man of peace, you are certainly welcome. If not, be gone, if you count your life dear," he replied firmly.

"I give you my word. I come in peace."

For a moment, the villager considered the stranger and his promise and then said, "Then, you are welcome."

With great effort Dunen began to get off his horse. Barely getting his leg over the side of his horse, total exhaustion overcame him causing him to fall to the ground and lose consciousness.

The villager carefully walked over to the stranger while cautiously looking around for trouble. He then knelt by his side. Curiously and carefully he examined him. He saw the wounds on his arms and the dry blood on his armor.

"Who are you, stranger? You have been in a great fight!" he said to himself with great interest. His eyes then widened with amazement as he saw a golden insignia of a lion on the breastplate. He recognised the emblem of the royal family of Teranda.

#

As Dunen began to wake up, he heard faint noises which he could not recognize. As he opened his eyes, he realized he was lying on a bed. The sound of children suddenly came to his attention and for a moment he was happy to hear their joyful cries.

Little by little his senses returned to him and fear began to take hold. Instinctively, he tried to get up but pain shot through his arms and his sides forcing him to stop. Relaxing his body, he looked around the place in which he found himself and guessed he was in a village hut. The only source of light in the dwelling found its way through the cracks in a window shutter. His sight cleared and adjusted to the partial darkness. The hut was a crude dwelling made of tree limbs and mortar. Quilted rugs of various sizes covered or hung on the walls. Dunen recognised the rugs by their woven patterns and guessed they belong to the villagers of the north.

Instantly he remembered the villager he had met in the forest. It was probably him who brought him to this village. A bit of relief came over Dunen, but he wondered: Which village? There were hundreds of villages. A map came to mind, one which he learned from his teachers. As he pictured the marked position of Teranda, thoughts of his father, mother and brother came to him and anguish immediately filled his heart. They were dead! Memories of the palace horror filled his mind as he turned his head into the pillow.

"No, no!" he cried with anguish. "Why did they die?"

He questioned their terrible death, which brought on a great feeling of loneliness. Lamenting his loss, he heard a voice, calm and overwhelming, entering his thoughts. Not a voice heard from without, but within him. Suddenly his anguish was forgotten, as the voice snatched all of his attention.

"Dunen," calming himself, listened with unbelief.

"Dunen. The covenant I made with your father I

make with you, if you obey my voice. The evil one grows stronger and seeks to destroy many. You will I send to overturn his devices and restore the city of your father. Be not troubled, I will be with you. Be of good courage and obey my voice."

As the presence of the voice faded away, Dunen felt an inner void and was left with his own thoughts.

"Was this a message from God?" he thought to himself. He was not sure. And what about retaking the city? How could this be? His father's army was destroyed and the enemy now resided safely behind the city's great walls.

"How can I take back the city? I'm alone!" he told himself.

Dunen's thoughts rose to God. "Lord God, how can I do this?"

'I will be with you.' Came the words to his mind again, not like before, but as a thought and reminder.

He was now the only heir to the throne and knew very well that it was his sacred duty and his father's will to regain the throne of his family.

Fearful and feeling unfit for the position, he fought against the idea. He did not wish to be king. His father had never trained him for this role; he would certainly fail. It was his brother's place, not his, he argued.

The opening of the door to the house broke his thoughts and caught his attention. As best as he could move, he looked at the visitor, but the bright light streaming from the open door made it difficult.

A village woman, moving softly and quietly as a dark shadow through the light, entered and approached him. In her hands, she carried a bowl covered with a towel. She stopped abruptly, realising her guest was awake. Regaining her composure and with humility she bowed before him.

"Forgive me if I have awakened you."

The woman remained bowed as Dunen looked on her.

"Do not be troubled, I was awake," he told her as he calmed himself and laid back his head.

The woman straightened up and walked gently over to the bedside.

"I have prepared for you a stew of vegetables and some bread."

"Thank you," he replied flatly.

She placed the stew on the table next to the bed and stepped back.

"Do you wish that I help you eat?" she said hesitantly.

"No," he replied coldly, although it would be easier he thought, but he wished to spend some more time alone.

"As you wish," she said kindly.

"In which village am I?"

"The village of Maarkaat."

This comforted him somewhat. Maarkaat was one of many villages in the Soloneb valley which had good relations with Teranda. He was safe with them, but for how long? He knew his enemies would now be searching to find and kill him.

"How long have I slept?" he asked, as the woman patiently waited on him.

"Two days."

Two days would give Lurion enough time to find him if he knew in which direction he went. Dunen felt he must quickly consider his next move, but what? Many things would have to be considered now that power in the region had changed.

"I would like to speak to the elder of your village, as soon as he is willing to see me," he said somewhat abruptly.

The woman answered, "He will be told."

"Thank you." Her smile caught his attention. She

was a simple woman. Her dark red hair was pushed back above her ears and tied behind her head. Her eyes were dark and alive. Soft and gentle was her face. Her calm but strong character attracted him. She bowed and retreated to the door. "I will not be far. If you desire anything, you may call. My name is Marani," she said and then left.

Alone, Dunen returned to his thoughts. Moving himself on the bed took effort. His wounds were treated and bandaged, but the pain was still present. He wondered how long before he would be fit to leave and where he would go or what he would do. His thoughts once again returned to the recent tragedy. His father and brother were killed before his eyes, but he knew nothing concerning his mother's fate. She could still be alive, he hoped. He knew he must find out for certain.

Sadness filled his heart and tears began to flow from his eyes. Burying his face in the pillow he cried and mourned for his family.

Chapter 3
THE LOST PIECE

The sky was clear as the midday sun shone brightly on a deserted field. Dense forest flanked closely on both sides of the field. In the distance, three horses and their riders emerged out of the forest in a furious gallop. Leading the three was Menfre, commander of king Favro's army. He was a tall man with a stern face, deep brown eyes and formidable build. The two others were mighty soldiers and personal guards. Long swords hung by their sides and dark green capes fluttered behind them from their swift ride. Their strong war-horses pounded the ground with their great hooves, sending dirt and rocks flying behind them.

After a short ride, the horsemen urged their mounts off the field to the opposite side and entered the dense forest. They slowed their pace as they travelled through the thick woods. Quickly they moved in and around the trees, knowing well their route. Coming to a small stream, they led their horses into the water. For a while they galloped in the shallow river splashing water on themselves and on every side. After trotting against the current for awhile, they then left the creek and entered the forest again. After a short ride, the terrain began to rise. The horses slowed their pace even more and were now trotting along. The riders earnestly urged the horses on. The climb ended on a small plateau and a large clearing could be seen a little further on. Breaking through the brush, the riders entered the open space where stood a large wooden house with a barn and stables enclosed completely by the forest. Servants and soldiers walked about the grounds, and stopped their chores to behold the arrivals. Several soldiers stood vigilantly before the door of the house.

As they arrived at the stables, the servants quickly took hold of the horses as they dismounted. "Prepare to leave as soon as possible," Menfre ordered one of his soldiers.

"Yes, sire," replied the soldier, and both soldiers immediately departed to execute his orders.

Inside the house, the entranceway opened to a large dining room. Several wooden tables and chairs were set in order in the room, where a hundred or so men would easily be accommodated. At the back of the room, a door led to the kitchen. A staircase to one side led up to rooms on a second floor. A huge fireplace brooded dark and unlit along one wall. Above the fireplace, on a marble shelf, lay small figurines of warhorses and famous men who had fought wars long ago. Flags with picturesque emblems of royal families hung along the walls.

On the far side, a woman stood by one of the few windows in the room. She was clothed in a burgundy dress with a golden belt around her waist. Her hair was long and brown with traces of white, telling her age. She was Lady Elena, queen of Teranda, and wife of the late Favro. Her face sagged with sadness from the recent events, and her movements were slow and weak. She turned her attention from the window to Menfre with a restrained hope of good news.

"Welcome, Menfre," she said calmly as possible.

"Thank you, my lady!" After bowing slightly, he walked over to a table which had cups, jugs and papers scattered all over.

Walking away from the window, she joined Menfre at the table. Her hopes died as Menfre showed no sign of good news.

With a slight huff, Menfre settled himself into one chair and poured himself a drink. He then drank, appreciating the refreshment after the long and hot ride.

She gathered her strength and asked, "What news have you?"

"No word of Dunen, my lady," he returned in a low tone, dismayed to give the unwanted news. "Neither have they found him. Blessed be God. Lurion has a great number of his army searching every inch of the country for him. It will not be long before they visit these parts."

Elena accepted the news with some hope.

"This of course places us in danger. We cannot remain any longer. We have waited long enough for Dunen to join us."

Elena disliked the thought of leaving the secret meeting lodge. If Dunen was truly alive, they all knew this would be the first place they should meet if in danger.

"If no one has found him," she said forcefully, "We must give him time."

"You are in danger!" Menfre almost shouted, "And I cannot lose ...," he trailed off and looked away, unwilling to show his pain over the death of his king and his son. His failure to protect the royal family weighed heavy on him. Feelings of guilt pierced his heart constantly.

Elena looked at him and understood his grief. Her husband was more than a king to Menfre, they were also close friends.

Elena reached out and laid her hand on his.

She knew they had given Dunen more than enough time.

"I will do as you say."

"Good," Menfre breathed a sigh of relief. He knew the queen's strong will very well and had lost many arguments with her in the past. And yet, he had never seen her weak as now. It pained him.

"I also have some bad news from the city. Many have been beheaded for resisting Lurion, and others fear Rondree and his soldiers. The people are watched closely, and few are allowed to enter or exit Teranda. He is slowly, and by false pretext, arresting noblemen who defy him or show any loyalty to us."

This angered Elena. "That wretched soul will certainly pay for what he has done. I know his desire is to give Teranda to Ernum, but he will not succeed as surely as I live."

"Perhaps not, my lady. Lurion would like the city for himself and Ernum cares not for it. He seeks the sword," Menfre stated gravely.

For a moment, they stared at each other with great concern, knowing well the serious implications if the Sword of Teranda fell into the hands of Ernum.

"Yes, I know. Let us pray he doesn't find it," she said as she calmed herself and focused her thoughts on important matters.

Menfre worried for his queen. Not only had she lost her loved ones but now was forced to take on all the great responsibility for the future of her people. He decided to change the subject.

"Another two hundred men have been added to our ranks. The men are in good spirits, but your presence among them would surely be welcomed."

"We will leave for camp today," she affirmed.

Menfre was glad and drank as he thought on certain matters. The room was quiet for a moment, as Elena also fell silent to her thoughts.

"I only pray that Dunen is alive," she finally said, not for the first time.

Menfre, roused by her doubt, quickly assured her. "I believe he is, my lady. Our God has assuredly spared his life and we will soon hear from him."

She looked at Menfre with some regret. "I pray the Lord forgive my lack of faith, dear Menfre. The loss of my husband and Tharan has dispirited me, and no word is given of Dunen."

"This is why I believe he yet lives!" Menfre said emphatically. "If he were dead, we would certainly have heard of it!"

Returning to her fears, she replied, "Indeed, it may be so, but he was wounded. The land is vast and I fear he lies dead on some unknown ground, never to be seen or found again!" she said and moved away trembling, returning to the window.

Menfre worried over the same thoughts.

"Why has God allowed this to happen?" she asked as she continued to look out the window.

Menfre breathed a sigh of nervousness. He had asked himself the same question and considered some unpleasant answers, which he was unwilling to reveal to anyone nor even consider it himself.

"Do not trouble yourself with such questions, my lady," he told her dryly and rose from his chair. "I must hurry and prepare for the journey."

"Very well," Elena said, not looking back.

Menfre bowed and left.

Staring out the window, Elena's thoughts reverted to Dunen, his unknown whereabouts troubling her. "Dunen, where are you? Oh Lord, my God. Keep him safe and return him to me, I beg you."

#

The door of the house opened and Marani moved out, walking backwards. She pushed the door wide open as Dunen slowly exited into the daylight. He quickly covered his eyes, unaccustomed to the light after residing in the darkened dwelling for several days.

Marani supported him as he limped along. The villagers immediately ceased their activities to look at Dunen for the first time since his arrival. Children ended their play as they watched with great curiosity and chattered with awe concerning him. Marani led him across the village centre. Some of the men along his path gave a welcoming smile and a slight bow. Dunen eyed them with great interest. It was the first time in all his life that he had entered a village of Soloneb.

These people were well-known for their courage in battle, their strength and skill in arms. They were also known for their love of God and their kindness. The men were of great size, height and muscular build, which commanded respect from all that stood before them. Their women were strong as well, but feminine and delicate despite their difficult life. Dunen and Marani arrived at the elder's home. Marani stopped and motioned that she would not accompany him further. He watched her go, then pushed the door open and entered. The hut was much larger than his and most others in the village. The floor was covered by many well-crafted rugs. At the far end of the room, an elderly man was seated cross-legged on pillows. His serene face looked up at Dunen. His eyebrows were thick and grey like his hair, his skin was dark and wrinkled with age. The walls were covered with various weapons of war, staffs and quilted images of victories and pacts.

"Come Dunen," he beckoned the young man with a wave of his thick weathered hand.

Dunen froze, surprised to hear his name, and then cautiously approached the man and bowed.

"You know who I am?" he asked.

The elder nodded. "Sit, sit, be comfortable," he urged him.

Dunen gathered a few pillows to him and, with some effort, sat before the elder.

"You are still in much pain I see," the elder noticed as he watched him carefully.

"Yes, but getting better by your good care," Dunen said as he settled down.

"I am glad. I met your father in earlier days. You were but a child at the time."

"Yes, I was taught of your meetings and agreements."

"He was a good man, and great in our eyes," the elder said, but immediately his peaceful face turned sombre. He bowed his head slightly and sadness crept over his face.

"I give you from my heart and from my people our deepest regret for the loss of your father and brother."

Dunen accepted the condolences and was touched by the elder's respect and interest in his family. "Thank you."

"It is of great sorrow to all who fear God," the elder said and spoke again after a moment of reflection, "You are welcome to stay with us as long as you wish. It is our honour to offer ourselves to you in gratitude for your father's grace and your grandfather's love toward us."

"Thank you again, you are most kind-" Dunen hesitated, not knowing his name.

The elder realised he didn't presented himself and said, "Forgive me, my friend. I am called Celkob."

Dunen had heard of him and was told that within these villages the men, with some exceptions, carried the name of their great forefather, as in this village the name was Ob.

"Thank you, Celkob, for your kindness. I will certainly stay, for I do not seem to have the strength to travel."

"Good," Celkob was glad, "You will be well cared for."

"But, I must warn you. Enemies seek my life and will soon search for me here."

"You will be safe with us, I assure you."

Dunen was relieved to hear this. "I must ask of you another favour."

Celkob quickly answered, "We are your servants! Ask and it shall be done. What does your heart desire?"

Dunen remembered the secret safe house his father had made. It was planned that in great peril, if anyone of his household or family advisers were in danger, they would hide at the secret lodge, but only for a short time. By now, Dunen believed, they were already gone.

"I must know if my mother lives. As I escaped, there was no time to find her. Do your people make frequent journeys to Teranda?"

"No. We villagers have little interest in the city, but I will send someone."

"Please do not endanger yourself or your people!"

Celkob reassured him, "Fear not my friend. It shall be done."

Dunen was happy to hear this and relaxed.

"What has happened, Dunen?" Celkob asked sensing that Dunen was at ease with him.

"A landlord of Teranda by the name of Lurion

usurped my father's throne. I believe he was helped by King Ernum of Dernak. Somehow he managed to bring a great number into the city and take us by surprise. I presume traitors amongst our people may also have helped him."

"Hmm. Truly a terrible event."

"I was not in the hall when it began; I was preparing to go to my father. Hearing the battle, I reached the hall to see my father and brother killed." Pausing, Dunen recollected the event and grief began to fill his heart, but quickly he subdued his emotions. "After that, I fled the city. I wandered in the woods until I was found by your villager."

"Yes. His name is Bilob. You will see him later. Hmm, the Lord be blessed for your safety, and yet, a terrible and sad day," Celkob nodded his head with concern.

Dunen studied the older man for a moment. From what he saw, he knew he sat before a great man, probably a mighty warrior of old. He also believed that this was a man who was kind, sensitive and full of wisdom.

"We live far from the cities, but we hear what is about. Evil days are once again upon us, Dunen. The wicked one is roaming about, seeking to turn many to his evil ways. He has succeeded with

Ernum and the city of Dernak, and now has taken Teranda."

Dunen agreed and was troubled to question why his father had overlooked the evil men rising within the city and their influence on others. How could his great advisors also fail to warn him? His pride and faith in his family was now shaken. It was his family's fault that the city had fallen.

"What will you do?" Celkob asked.

"I am not certain. I must first know if my mother lives. Then I must know what happened and if there are still any left loyal to my father's house."

Celkob nodded in agreement.

"Yes, this is good. But you must stay and strengthen yourself, for I am sure a long and difficult road lies before you."

Dunen considered Celkob's serious and wise warnings and knew he was right. He wasn't sure what would happen in the days to come, but he knew it would involve him deeply.

"I thank you again."

"It is our joy and duty. Be of good cheer, you are among friends," Celkob replied with a comforting smile.

As he felt glad for their support, Dunen realized it was God who led him to Maarkaat. The thought encouraged him and he thanked the Lord and was grateful for the needed care and friendship.

#

Inside the throne hall of the royal palace of Teranda, the high and heavy wooden doors opened. On either side of the doors, a great stone statue stood on their pedestals, facing the throne at the other end. The left statue was in the image of the great warrior Teranda, and the other was of King Anunden, father to King Favro. Both were sculpted in their armor and holding the infamous sword of Teranda made of glass, named after its first owner.

Through the doors entered a tall and broad shouldered man dressed in a robe of dark purple and green. His face was gaunt and grim. His eyes were piercing and his nose short and pointed. His gaze was ruthless and cold.

He briskly walked across the lengthy hall with great imposing strides. On the throne, Lurion sat, tapping the floor before him with his black and silver sceptre. He was an overweight man and with a forehead knotted with concern. His eyes gave away his wicked and deceitful character.

"Ah, my dear Rondree, what good news do you bring me?" Lurion called out as he forced a pleasant smile.

Rondree marched up several steps of the throne platform and gave a short bow on one knee.

"We have not found Dunen as yet," he answered bluntly.

Lurion's mild appearance quickly vanished to the news and then turned his gaze away with concern and irritation.

"I have doubled the search and am looking to the north in the wooded areas of the tribal territories, my king," Rondree continued.

Lurion quickly burst at him. "I am no king unless he is dead!" He then calmed down and continued, "Opposition will increase if his head does not hang outside the gate."

"He will be found, my lord," Rondree assured him.

Lurion gave him a doubtful stare and again turned his gaze elsewhere as he considered the situation. "What of Lady Elena and her army?"

"We are not sure of her whereabouts," Rondree replied. "Some say she waits for Dunen at a secret location. As for Favro's army, they are presently one-third our size, but grow in number each passing day."

Rondree's report agitated Lurion further.

"If our search for Dunen remains fruitless, we must

consider attacking the army and assure our victory," Rondree advised after a long silence.

"Yes, I know, Rondree," Lurion replied, considering his words. "But we must be careful. Our master will not be too happy with us if we tarry to secure the throne and find his precious sword. I can assure you," he said sarcastically as he revealed not only his dislike for Ernum but his fear of him.

Rondree also feared Ernum and didn't like to consider the thought of failing him either.

"The search continues. If the sword is in the city, we will find it."

"Huh!" Lurion said doubtfully.

"You are sure that Favro did not give the sword to Dunen in his last moment?" Rondree dared to ask.

"It was not the sword of Teranda! It is well known that Favro refused to use it. And it did not save him, did it?" Lurion retorted fervently.

Rondree agreed with him. If Favro was using the sword of Teranda, he would still be alive and king of the city. The sword's legend was well known. It made its wielder invincible. No other sword could match its metal and some claimed it was made by God, to guard the Garden of Eden. Those who wielded in battle won many victories, but Rondree feared a darker purpose why Ernum wanted the sword.

"We will continue to search the Palace and question the people. As for their army, we have the numbers to defeat them when the time comes."

"Do not be so sure, my dear Rondree. I will not be at peace till Dunen is dead or his army destroyed. Do you understand?"

"They will be defeated," Rondree said confidently.

"Then go my servant. And do so quickly. The sooner our claim is sure, the sooner we can rejoice and be merry," Lurion exhorted him.

Rondree bowed quickly, and left the room with an eager pace to make good his words.

Lurion watched him go with a hint of distrust. Nervously, he fondled his sceptre.

#

Four horses and their riders galloped along a dusty winding path. It was a sunny day and shadows of nearby trees crossed the way. The horsemen were soldiers of Lurion's army. Their armor was dark grey, and silver straps crossed their waists and breastplates, and each wore metal helmets.

Far up in a tree, a sentinel from the village of Maarkaat watched them go by. Hidden by the foliage, he rested on a small wooden platform. He quickly grabbed a bow and arrow. Raising himself, he turned to shoot in the same direction in which the horsemen travelled. With a powerful tug, he pulled the bowstring and let go the arrow, sending it to an unseen destination.

Within the village of Maarkaat, a villager ran quickly to the tent of Celkob and entered. Inside, Celkob was seated, eating his midday meal. At the coming of the villager, he stopped and looked up. The villager gave a respectful bow and said:

"Soldiers of the city approach the village."

Celkob's eyes widened with great interest. "Hide our friend. They are not to see him."

The villager immediately obeyed. Celkob rose from his seat. Taking his staff and praying to the Lord for guidance, he left his home.

Outside, within the village square, the villagers continued their affairs as if nothing was new. Celkob moved towards the centre as he beheld, far off, the horsemen coming.

The horsemen slowed their pace as they entered the outer perimeter of the village. Moving along, they looked at the villagers with disdain. Their leader, on noticing Celkob alone in the centre, moved his horse towards him, stopping only a few feet from the old man. With a stern and disgusted gaze, the leader looked down over his sweating horse to the elderly chieftain. Celkob raised a smile and welcomed the strangers.

"Welcome to Maarkaat. I am Celkob, chief of this village. How can we, your servants, be of service?"

The captain of the four responded coldly as he examined the village, "We are soldiers of King Lurion of Teranda. He bids thee peace and prosperity. By his order we seek a man, a criminal, who has escaped the city. Have you seen any stranger about your village of late?"

The villagers stopped their activity to listen and waited anxiously on the answer of their leader.

"A criminal? What has this man done?" Celkob asked.

"He is an enemy of the king. A rebel against the authority of our sovereign lord," the soldier answered impatiently.

Celkob paused a moment as if reflecting. "No. We have seen no strangers."

The captain watched Celkob carefully and doubted his words.

"Are you sure?"

With a firm expression, Celkob retorted, "I assure you, we have not seen any strangers about our village in these last few days."

With disbelief, the captain moved back in his saddle and relaxed his gaze. "Very well, then. If any outsiders come by this way, it would be wise to send us word."

"We have no dealings with the city dwellers." Celkob informed him.

Ignoring his comment, the soldier spoke loudly so that all the villagers could hear and said, "A great reward is given to whoever will help us find him!"

Returning to his conversation with Celkob, the captain informed him with a hateful and ominous tone, "And woe to those that shelter him!"

"You will be told of any stranger coming here," Celkob assured him calmly.

Giving him a hateful stare, the captain jerked his horse into a turn and led his men into a gallop as they left the village.

Celkob watched them go with relief, but was also greatly concerned by the visit. The quiet tension in the village broke into much chatter and discussions. Bilob and two other men walked over to Celkob with worried faces.

"You chose your words wisely," Bilob said proudly.

"Yes. Dunen is not a stranger," Celkob smiled.

The villagers laughed at deceiving the soldiers.

"Do you think he believed you?" Bilob asked.

"These men are hard to read. They trust none. I am sure they will return," he answered.

"Then we must be ready."

"Yes. We must." Celkob agreed seriously.

When Dunen was certain that the soldiers were gone, he emerged from his hut and quickly walked over to Celkob. Most of his bandages were now removed and his strength had increased enough for him to walk unaided.

"They came for me?" Dunen asked.

"Yes." Celkob answered.

"I told you I could endanger your people. I must leave."

"No!" Celkob said forcefully. "And where would you go?"

"Yes! Where would you go?" Bilob repeated.

Dunen knew he could not answer that question knowing very little of the current situation of his people.

"Be not troubled, my friend. Stay with us, for it is needful that you be amongst us. The Lord will watch over us, and we need not be afraid," Celkob responded with assurance and then added, "These men would have come no matter. You will change nothing to leave."

"Yes! Hear him. Stay with us!" Bilob urged.

Dunen found Bilob's eager desire for him to stay strange but heart warming.

"You don't understand," Dunen protested. "If these soldiers have any suspicion of my presence, they will return and with great force. Lurion's army can destroy your village with little effort."

"Let them come! They will taste the steel of Maarkaat!" Bilob bellowed proudly and his two companions fisted their chests in agreement.

"Do not listen to them. They are young and have not seen the first wars," Celkob said as he gave them a stern look.

Their courage faded a little as Bilob and his fellow tribesmen remembered the old stories that almost destroyed all the tribes of Soloneb.

"Then I will have watchmen sent, my father. They will warn us of their coming even to a day," Bilob advised Celkob.

Celkob nodded with agreement. "Do so."

Bilob and the two tribesmen left immediately.

"Celkob," Dunen wanted to say more but Celkob interrupted.

"Hear me. I perceive this is God's doing. We have a part to play."

Dunen considered his words for a moment and

then unhappily nodded his acceptance.

"You must gather your strength and be prepared for your time to act," Celkob advised him.

"I am still weak," Dunen admitted.

"Good, be comforted. The Lord will manifest his will in due time. Be patient," Celkob urged him.

Dunen nodded reluctantly.

"Thank you," Dunen said gratefully, and yet he doubted the old man's decision. He left Celkob and return to his house.

Celkob watched him go, but concern spread across his face. Trouble was brewing, and he knew he must plan for difficult times ahead. If Dunen did not regain the throne of Teranda, peace would be lost between both people.

Dunen stopped at the door of his house and hesitated to enter. Changing his mind, he headed off amid the houses of the village and toward the forest that encircled it. Entering the solitude of the forest, he strolled amidst the trees, following a well-trodden path as he thought on his present situation. The calm and warm day and the tall majestic trees turned his attention from his problems, and he began to enjoy the stroll. Nature had always lifted his spirit. In the distance, the sound of waterfalls caught his attention and curiosity led him to follow the water's soft invitation. It reminded him of his fishing along the river of Teranda's valley, and wished he could be by its peaceful side again. How far away those days seemed to him now, and how much changed in a few short days!

Dunen's walk ended at the riverbank. As he left the forest, the view opened to a small waterfall coming from the hillsides. The stream was a hundred or so feet across and moved slowly by. Great mountains in the distance draped across the horizon, mountains like the ones beside his city, beautiful and majestic. The splendour overcame him and lightened his heart. The thought of God came naturally to his mind as he considered His great creation.

Dunen walked to a huge rock protruding from the ground and sat on it. This was the first time for days that he felt comfortable enough to talk to God. Considering the great power in His creation, a question came to Dunen's mind. Why did God not warn or protect his father and brother? Why did they die and why was he spared? Both were godly men; their walk with Him was irreproachable.

"Why Lord?" Dunen asked God. He could not

understand! And yet, deep down, he knew that the fault lay with them. Since the sin of Adam and Eve, the earth has seen the result of mankind's disobedience against God. Dunen could only hope to learn the reason in due time, if the Lord willed that he know. Considering this grave situation, he felt that for the sake of many and for himself, he must strengthen his fellowship with God and acquire His guidance in the things he must do next. Lifting his head and looking at the beautiful landscape, Dunen understood that in all this great creation, he was to be used for some purpose, great or small.

A large splash coming from the river not far from his position interrupted his thoughts. The splash being too large to be made by a fish, aroused Dunen's curiosity. He raised himself from the rock and climbed on it. Looking over a hedge of bushes that had partially obstructed his view of the river to his right, he searched for the cause of the splash.

In the river, he saw a woman bathing. Buried beneath the water, he could see her through the ripples. The clear water revealed that she was not bare. She soon emerged out of the water, puffing for air and wiping the dripping water from her face. Shortly she plunged again beneath the waves.

When she emerged once more not far from him, Dunen recognised her to be Marani.

As she looked towards the shore, she saw Dunen and let out a gasp of surprise. "Oh!" she burst out.

"I am sorry to have frightened you," he said, moving off his rock and drawing closer to the water. Marani waded slowly towards him in the shallow water and came up onto the shore.

"You do not have to come out," he told her.

"It is all right. I came only to be refreshed."

She moved to a nearby place where a towel lay. She sat and dried herself with it. Dunen joined her, but paid no attention to her as he returned his gaze to the scenery. "It is a beautiful day," he said.

Marani stopped from arranging her wet clothes to notice his remark and also notice his change of mood. Dunen, remarking her silence, turned to catch her staring at him. She turned away, shyly.

"I'd like to thank you for taking care of me," Dunen said as he considered her help.

"It was my duty," she replied with a little smile.

"Oh, I see." Dunen noticed her sly smile. "I hope I wasn't difficult."

"You were as men are," she answered with a giggle and Dunen laughed.

As she turned away, Dunen looked at her and

carefully noticed her features.

Marani had soft cheeks and the dark eyes filled with sensitivity and curiosity. Her skin was slightly darker, rarely seen among the princesses and noble ladies he knew, an olive tone that shone, now even more by the water from her swim. Her young and strong character gave Dunen a desire he had not felt for a long time. Her simplicity, and most of all her friendliness, attracted him. Realising he was staring at her, he turned away, feeling embarrassed.

"The city Teranda is surrounded by mountains like this. Have you ever been to Teranda?"

"Only as a child," she replied.

"Well, you should go some day and see it again," Dunen urged her and added, "It has changed."

"Maybe someday."

As he turned to look at her again, she raised herself to her feet.

"I must return to the village. I have chores to do."

Dunen got to his feet as well.

"I must also return. Will you lead me back?"

"Yes," she answered.

They left the stream behind and entered the woods using another path.

Walking along, she asked him, "What will you do

now that your enemies seek you?"

"I am not certain. I have told Celkob that I will remain until I am fit to leave. Then I must seek word of my mother's welfare."

"The throne of your father, will you try to regain it?"

Dunen became nervous at the question. They all expected him to take back his father's throne, but he felt unsure of himself. He had always thought his brother would be king, but now the right and responsibility fell on him.

"I do not know," he could only answer as he looked away from her eyes. He felt guilty and a failure for his lack of decisiveness.

Marani only nodded.

"Your people are in danger," Dunen said.

"How?" she asked with great concern.

"If Lurion's men find that I am here, they will come and destroy the village."

Shouts within the forest interrupted their conversation.

"What is this?" Dunen asked worriedly.

"The village men are sporting with the fight," Marani explained. "Would you like to see them?"

"Yes, I would," Dunen said with great interest.

"Come."

She led him away from the path and walked deeper into the forest. After a small trek, they came to a clearing. A short rock wall ran along the border of the clearing. The corners of the wall did not join, allowing an entrance to the clearing.

A dozen village men were in a circle looking attentively at two other villagers fighting with swords. They shouted with excitement, urging them on and giving instructions to their favourites. Dunen and Marani entered the clearing. Dunen watched with amazement. He had heard of the villagers fierce fighting in battle and was happy to see them perform.

The size of the villagers was above the average man in height and width. Their skill in arms added to their abilities, making them opponents to be feared by all. Dunen wondered how the city soldiers would fare up against these fighters. At this moment, one of the fighters was able to move his sword and stab at his opponent's chest and win the fight. Dunen realised that the swords were blunted, and only bruises would be left after a contest. The villagers cheered for the winner, and then Bilob entered the circle.

"Good, my brother. Very good," Bilob praised the winner. Turning around, he spotted Dunen and

Marani.

"Ah, Dunen! A welcome surprise."

The villagers turned to look, and immediately gave their visitor a short bow of welcome. He in like manner responded.

"Come join us. I hear that the Terandians are excellent in war and have mastered the sword fairly well," Bilob said.

Dunen smirked at the weak evaluation of Terandian fighting, but for a friendly challenge he happily joined them.

"On behalf of the Terandians, I am honoured by your words," Dunen replied.

"Will you sport with me, that we may see your methods and skill?" Bilob asked enthusiastically and the others also became excited of the duel.

Dunen didn't mind; this would also help him exercise his healed muscles.

"Very well, my friend."

The villagers became very excited and gave space for the combatants. Marani was the only one unhappy with the duel and knew she could not stop it. Watching her brother fight with Dunen gave her mixed emotions.

Bilob handed Dunen a sword and then gave each other space. Dunen was disappointed in his sword as he handled it, finding it heavier than the city swords. Taking several practice swings, he noted that the handle was larger than normal and made it harder for him to hold. The sword was also badly balanced and would take further effort to control. These were disadvantages for him and would require more effort on his part to compensate for the crude sword.

Immediately they started. Dunen was calm and his posture relaxed from the many years of training and compertitions. Bilob moved his position quickly but with hard steps. Dunen began to judge his style and at the same time consider certain strategies. They struck at each other on several occasions, testing each other's moves and counter-moves. Dunen knew if the fight were long, he would have to use both hands to wield the heavy sword, which would further limit his moves. Bilob launched a low strike across the side, but Dunen deflected his aim and moved around to strike in return, sending Bilob back. Bilob was surprised as well as bothered not to have succeeded in his strike, and began to add emotion to his fight. Bilob sent several quick cuts and strikes toward Dunen's chest, only to be blocked and receive instead a hit on his left leg. Bilob, stunned by the blow, jumped back.

The villagers were silent and tense like stone figures as they gained respect for Dunen's swordsmanship.

At first Bilob held back his strength. Now seeing Dunen's skill, he struck back with full force, pushing Dunen back and finding occasion to hit him also on the leg. Some of the villagers cheered, but quickly fell silent. Dunen realised he could not win by force. If anything, he must use strategy taught to him by the masters of his people. He then moved forward, striking violently, causing Bilob to retreat. Bilob, surprised for a moment by the powerful comeback, finally resisted the onslaught by returning strong blows and began to push forward.

This is what Dunen expect him to do. Retreating slowly, Bilob continued his forceful push. At this moment, Dunen faked a blow to the leg and moved his sword up towards the chest. Bilob perceived the move and pushed his sword to Dunen's chest, turning his body parallel to his opponent's sword. Dunen's sword missed the mark and Bilob struck home at the heart. Dunen froze at the move and the fight was over.

The villagers cheered for Bilob. Dunen stood

surprised but at the same time interested in what Bilob had done.

"You have fought well, my friend," Dunen said breathing hard by the exertion.

Bilob was happy at the compliment, but was also impressed by Dunen.

"I am honoured. And what has been said of the Terandian warriors is true. They are a match indeed," Bilob replied.

Dunen smiled with gratitude at his words.

"Would you dine at my home tonight, my friend?"

"Yes, it would be a pleasure and an honour to do so."

With his great big hand, Bilob slapped Dunen on the shoulder with joy. The others also enjoyed the match, but were also happy with the new friendship.

Marani was relieved and followed the men as they all walked towards the village. She was happy and a felt excited to hear of his visit. All along the way, the men talked with Dunen about sword fighting and questioning him about his knowledge and experience.

Chapter 4
THE CAMP OF FELLOWSHIP

Far south, in the immense forest of Forwilda, the Terandian army camped on a large open field. The great trees of Forwilda surrounded the camp like a huge curtain. The field was filled with hundreds of tents, campfires, horses and men moved about their business. At the centre of the field, larger tents housed the captains of the army.

A trumpet sounded within the camp and all the soldiers stopped to look to the northern part of the camp.

In the distance, a train of horsemen rode into camp. Word spread quickly as news of the queen's arrival was proclaimed from soldier to soldier. The soldiers left their duties as they gathered to the sides of the main path leading to the centre pavilions. They began to shout and wave with great welcomes as they followed after her. Elena, with great joy, waved back at them.

"Long live the queen! Long live the queen!" the soldiers shouted with fervour and with great joy.

Ever since the day King Favro had chosen Elena to be his queen, the soldiers admired her kindness and wisdom, but most of all for her great faith in

God the Creator.

The riders ended their journey near the tents. Three of the captains exited the royal tents and came to welcome the queen. The queen raised her hand for silence. The camp quieted as the soldiers obeyed her immediately. She composed herself and looked around at the soldiers.

"Your welcome has greatly lifted my spirit. Moreover, your courage and loyalty for our people and our God is an unspeakable joy to behold and I am honoured to be in such company. The Lord forbid that this day ever fade from my memory."

The soldiers in unison cheered their queen even louder and then quickly went silent to hear her again.

"I know that you have all worked and suffered much in these last days, and have shown your deepest love towards our people, and your desire to reclaim our beloved city," Elena said with admiration. "My prayers most surely cry up to our God for each of you, and I know the Lord will grant us victory over our enemies."

Exhorted by her words, the soldiers responded with a hearty cheer and with much shouting. The queen happily looked on them, blushing with pride.

A servant helped her dismount from her horse, and she was led towards the command tent amid the continual shouts of "Long live Queen Elena!" The shouting diminished only after she and the captains were within the tent, and then slowly the camp returned to normal.

The large tent was furnished with a great wooden table in the middle, with chairs placed around it. Trunks were spread along the tent walls. All over the table, maps and drinking cups were scattered. The tent was well illuminated by the sun passing through its thin fabric.

A servant quickly helped the queen to remove her riding cloak as the captains placed themselves around the table and sat down.

Manru was a tall and lean man with light hair. He captained the archers. Shadly, on the other hand, was a large muscular man with earth-brown hair. He captained the foot soldiers. Danar was the smallest of them all, but no less in might than his fellows. He captained the horsemen. Each of them had shown their great courage in battle and their loyalty to their king.

Elena, brushing her dress in place, came to the table and sat at the head. Menfre stood beside her.

"I cannot recall when I have been welcomed in

such a manner," the queen told her captains as she considered her soldier's cheers.

"You are greatly beloved, my lady," stated Shadly.

Elena returned a smile. "They seem to be in good spirits."

"Yes, my lady. Even more now that you are with us," Danar added.

"God bless their souls."

"Well, my lady. What news do you bring us?" asked Manru.

"No news concerning my son," she replied, hiding her sadness and remaining strong.

The cheer of the last few moments faded from the captains, as they feared for Dunen's life.

"But we have word that neither have our enemies found him," Menfre quickly added.

The captains sighed with some relief.

"What then must we do?" asked Shadly.

"As long as Lurion does not find us, we will also continue to search for Dunen," Elena replied.

"No disrepect, my lady, but Lurion surely knows where we are," Manru offered, as the others agreed. "He has many eyes and nothing escapes him. He has not come up against us because it suits his purpose."

"Well, then, it serves our purpose as well, does it

not?"

"Yes, of course, but we must prepare another plan if Dunen is not found," Shadly suggested with sensitivity for Elena's feelings.

"Indeed, we must be prepared. The men will lose courage if we tarry too long," Danar confirmed.

All of the men looked on Elena. She hesitated to answer, not willing to put aside her hopes for Dunen's return, but she could not forget her city and her people.

"Forgive me; I lack judgment in these matters. You may proceed with your plans, if you so believe them to be necessary."

The captains relaxed, happy to have her permission, but also respecting her gentle humility.

"Thank you, my lady." said Menfre.

"What is our present situation?" the queen asked.

"We have three thousand from the original guard and several hundred who have joined us and are being trained. Our numbers are not what they once were years ago and good soldiers are hard to find," Shadly informed her.

"Yes, I know. A fault of my husband's I believe," Elena said shamefaced.

No one returned any comment, knowing the discussions and criticisms concerning the late

King's unwise decisions in the last years of a peaceful reign.

"Our supplies are plenty and many friends continue to give willingly, even at their great peril," Manru said.

"Blessed people, the Lord reward them a hundredfold," Elena prayed with gratitude.

"Many more join us every day, but I fear we will never equal the size and strength of Lurion's army, nor have we enough time to train them."

The men fell silent and Elena knew they left out the most important question.

"How many men do they have?" she asked.

"We are informed that he has twice our numbers," Shadly said.

Elena looked at the captains while controlling her dismay. "Then we have no hope."

"It is difficult to judge," Shadly added.

"Why?" She quickly asked.

"We know little of their army." Shadly explained.

"We know nothing of Rondree, the captain of Lurion's army, nor his strategies in battle," Menfre informed her.

"We have seen them fight in the city, my lady, but not on the field." Danar added.

Elena looked at her captains, hoping to learn what

they really believed, but found nothing.

She turned to Menfre, "What is your opinion, Menfre?" She asked.

Menfre thought for a moment and then replied, "I say we can win the day."

Elena did not show the men how relieved she was. The captains hid their fears from the queen and agreed with Menfre.

"I trust that you will give us the victory," she said confidently. "And let us not forget that our God stands with us. He will not fail us," she reminded them.

All the men gave their hearty assurance of their faith.

"Very well, then. We will take the time God allots us and do what we can," Elena said encouragingly.

The men nodded in agreement.

"And fear not, we will continue to seek for Dunen and retrieve news of the city," Menfre promised her.

"Thank you, Menfre." The queen rose from her chair and the captains rose as well. "If you will excuse me, I am weary and hungry from the journey. I have done more riding in recent days than any queen should ever want or deserve," she said with some humour.

The captains chuckled.

"We are happy to have you among us, my lady," said Manru, with the others giving assent.

"We will make your stay among us as pleasant as possible," added Danar.

"You may find me hard to please, Danar," Elena said, and all laughed. "I thank you and I hope to be of some service."

"Your presence alone is all we could ask for, my lady," said Shadly.

The queen smiled at the compliment and turned to leave, followed by a servant.

The captains bowed respectfully as she left the tent. Once alone, the captains turned to face Menfre.

"You've promised her victory when we cannot be sure of anything?" Shadly said unhappily.

"Even if all goes well in battle, we would be lucky for a truce," Danar added frustratingly.

"She is our Queen!" Menfre said as he gave his captains a stern gaze, "She deserves our confidence."

His men understood and felt a little ashamed. None of them wanted their beloved queen to lose faith or be discouraged.

"We will do our best to win this victory," Menfre urged his captains.

"And if perchance we win," Shadly said sceptically, "Do you believe we will have enough men to take the city?"

Menfre gravely looked at his captains and unwillingly answered, "No."

Chapter 5
THE UNWELCOMED KING

On an early afternoon in Maarkaat, two villagers, dusty from a long journey, rode into the village. Some saluted as the traveller's hurriedly moved to Celkob's tent. They dismounted, leaving their horses beside the house, and quickly entered. Not long after, the same two riders and Celkob exited the hut. Hurriedly they walked to Dunen's hut with concerned looks. Celkob knocked at his door.

"Dunen, it is Celkob; I must speak with you."

"A moment, please." After a short wait, Dunen appeared at the door. He quickly noticed the riders. "These have come from the city and have some news for you," Celkob reported.

Dunen became excited and was eager to hear what they had to say.

"We arrived at the city walls and found them barred and guarded," one of the riders began. "We asked to enter, but the guards questioned us about our purpose. We told them we came as usual to buy goods for our tribe. They would not allow us to enter, and told us it may be long before we would be allowed to trade. And so we returned. We did not wish to speak to the common people outside, for fear we would speak to the wrong people and be exposed."

Celkob nodded with agreement. "You have done well."

"Yes. Thank you," Dunen said, forcing a smile, although very disappointed. He felt downcast to have gained no further knowledge of his mother or of his people.

With this the two men bowed and left. Bilob, seeing the conversation from afar off, drew closer and heard the story.

Dunen felt he could not continue his plans unless he knew what had happened to his mother.

"Celkob, I must go to the city and know for myself what has happened to my mother and my friends!"

"What? And be captured? That would be foolish! You will certainly be discovered and killed!" Celkob answered quickly, and with great displeasure at the thought.

"I see no other way! It is where I will find all my answers," Dunen responded.

"Are there others outside the city that we can question?" Bilob asked.

"No," Dunen answered. "Not who would be able to tell all that I need to know, and who can be trusted. I must go and enter the city."

"And how do you plan to do this?" asked Celkob.

"There is a secret way into the city that will bring me inside without alerting the guards," Dunen said, looking thoughtful. "It is safe."

"This is not the time to take great risks," Celkob told him firmly.

"Fear not. I am not so foolhardy. I will be safe." he reassured him.

Celkob and Bilob looked at each other and knew they could no more dissuade Dunen from his desires.

"If you must, I will go with you," said Bilob decidedly.

Dunen was about to disagree, but saw that Bilob would not be deterred. In fact, he was glad to have his help and companionship.

"It is good that Bilob go with you, but I disagree with your plan," Celkob said seriously. "Your city and all that are free depend on your well-being, and for you to go into the lion's den I believe to be very dangerous."

"I will be very careful, Celkob," he said placing his hand on his shoulder. "I must leave immediately."

"I will go to prepare for the journey; tomorrow we leave," Bilob said.

Dunen nodded, and Bilob ran off leaving him alone

with Celkob.

"I can do no more now than to pray for your safe return," Celkob said unhappily and then walked away.

Dunen watched him go and felt sad to reject his advice. For the little time he had spent with Celkob, he had found a place in his heart for him, and did not wish to disappoint him. But Dunen realised there was no other way to gather word of his mother and the state of the kingdom. He felt at the same time that he should begin to act on the Lord's will.

Returning to his house, he began to contemplate the journey. As he sat on the bed and planned his journey, he decided to disguise himself in case of any unexpected encounters along the way. He was wondering what he should wear for the journey and what other things to bring, when suddenly the door flung open and Marani hurried inside, halting abruptly as if caught by surprise. She looked concerned and yet, at the same time, she tried to mask it.

"Bilob has told me of your journey to Teranda, and - I came to say farewell," she said with difficulty.

Dunen saw that she wanted to say more, but feared to do so. From his first day in Maarkaat, he knew she was interested in him.

"Thank you, Marani. Do not fear, our God will be with us," he told her confidently.

"Yes, of course," she returned hesitantly even though her troubled heart yearned to dissuade him from his plans.

"I know your prayers will be heard, and we will return safely," he said trying to reassure her.

"God will bless your journey and will give you what you seek. Farewell, Dunen." Marani said as she offered a weak smile of assurance then bowed and left.

Dunen could see she feared for him, and his heart was touched by her love, but he forced those thoughts aside, knowing that he must give his full attention to the difficult decisions he would have soon have to make.

Early next morning, Dunen stepped outside his home and saw Celkob, with some relatives of Bilob, standing and talking beside two horses in the village square. The Soloneb villagers bred great and strong horses, and Dunen was pleased to have the occasion to ride one. It would take about two days to reach Teranda and they would be well supplied for the journey. Dunen joined the villagers and gave his bag to Bilob, who placed it on his horse. Last words were exchanged and farewells given, then immediately the two men mounted their horses and, with a wave, they were off. Dunen noticed Marani was nowhere in sight at his departure and felt a little sad for leaving without saying, farewell.

Along the way, Bilob and Dunen spoke much about the trip and about Teranda. They decided on Bilob's advice to take another route to Teranda, a mountain pass rarely used. It would lengthen their trip, but would certainly keep them from meeting any unwanted foes. At midday, they stopped for a quick lunch.

As soon as they were on their way, the land began to rise. For a distance, they rode below the mountain tree line, but it was not long before they were high enough to see the countryside. As they continued their journey, they arrived on the side of one mountain range which led to a small valley. The valley was called Darr An. Several battles had taken place at the outer end of the valley, when Teranda began to grow in repute in its earlier days.

Evening came, and they camped not far from the path. After dinner, Dunen and Bilob rested near the fire. Dunen reached for his sword and pulled it out of its scabbard. It glittered with streaks of silver and red from the fire's light. Bilob's eyes widened with awe as he gazed at the weapon.

"Is this the sword of Teranda? " Bilob asked, as he looked on it with great admiration.

"No, it is not," Dunen answered. "Long ago, my father hid the sword and I believe he alone knew where it was hidden. He trusted no one with his secret. And now that he is dead, it may never be found."

"Hmm," Bilob nodded with great disappointment. "We have heard much of this sword. They say it was created by the hand of God himself and given to the angel of the garden! Do you believe this?"

"I do not know. I was a child when my father wielded it in battle. Some say it is true, others could only say how it easily it cut its foes asunder."

Bilob marvelled as he imagined the stories of the sword and nodded his head with respect as he recalled the great tales of old. "Nevertheless, your sword is also magnificent!"

"This was my father's sword. He gave it to me just before he died," Dunen said as he remembered how he had received it. He looked at its mirrored steel with sadness, wishing to see it in the hands of his father.

Bilob saw his sadness. "Forgive me, my friend."

Dunen broke away from his reflection and comforted his friend, "I am well."

The villagers were excellent fighters but not sword-makers, Dunen thought. They made their own swords, but style and design were not attainable with their skills. The Terandian swords were known for their lightweight and hard steel, which made them choice weapons. They were designed to fit perfectly in the owner's hand, with the hilt offering good protection. Most of all, the metal was balanced to require the least effort when wielding it. Carvings along the blade and handle included the family name, symbols and words of wisdom.

Dunen lifted the sword before him and admired it. Bilob's scrutiny drew his attention to curved indentations along the blade and near the hilt.

"What are those cuts?" Bilob asked, pointing to the blade.

"They have a purpose that I cannot say, but you will know soon," Dunen answered.

Bilob raised his eyebrows with curiosity, wondering about their mysterious purpose and what Dunen meant when he said he would know soon.

Dunen then yawned, feeling tired from the tense

day.

"We should sleep now. We have a difficult path tomorrow and a rough ride."

"Nor will I tarry," Dunen assured him. "The ride has been hard on my sore bones."

Bilob gave back the sword and lay down on his bed of blankets.

"Good night, my friend. The Lord keep your heart in peace," Bilob said while laying down his head.

"Good night to you, Bilob. The Lord bless your rest," Dunen responded.

In a short time, all was quiet, but for the sound of the fire and the growing rumble of Bilob's snoring. Dunen placed his sword back in the scabbard and laid it aside. Looking up into the clear night, he marvelled at the countless bright and twinkling stars that spread across the sky.

"How great is thy power, God of the heavens," he thought, his spirit lifted by the sight. "Your might is past knowing and thy wisdom never reached."

The night sky always amazed Dunen, giving him great comfort that God was the creator of it all. This made him take a time of worship and was glad to do so. Finally feeling tired, he lay down on his blankets and soon fell asleep as he closed his eyes to the stars.

The two travellers awoke early in the morning, had a short breakfast, gathered their possessions and resumed the trail. It was hard going down the mountainside. Some places were steep and had to be descended carefully, which proved slow and wearisome. Dunen understood why others would not tread this way. Several hours later, they came midway down the mountain to level ground. The narrow plateau was a welcome difference. They trotted slowly along, giving the horses a change of pace, and admiring the landscape.

"The half is done," Bilob announced.

"Good. We may go-" Dunen's words trailed off the moment he spotted a man far up the path.

Bilob, who was leading and looking back at Dunen, noticed his concerned expression and turned to look ahead. Dunen immediately pulled up his hood to cover his head and hide his face. They slowly approached an old man who was seated on a rock beside the path. The old man looked up at the riders and raised himself to his feet. His cloak hung to the ground, and he held a smooth dark walking stick. A hood partly covered his head, but his face was clearly visible. His face was bearded with skin wrinkled by age and yet still manifested strength. His eyes were piercing and deep, as if he could look through a person. The riders approached him and halted. Bilob spoke first.

"Good day, old man, and peace be unto you. Can we be of any help?" he asked politely.

"I thank you, but I need nothing that our blessed Creator has not provided," the man replied calmly.

"Do you live in the mountains that we find you so far from the valley?" asked Bilob, finding it strange that this old man was up here alone, with no horse or donkey in sight.

"No. My home is not nigh, nor do I live in these parts."

Bilob and Dunen found the old man strange, and his answer made them more suspicious than ever.

"Well, then, a wanderer you may be, ay?" Bilob suggested.

"Even as wind is driven by God, I also am led here to speak to you," the old man said as he raised his staff towards Dunen. "Dunen, son of Favro," he ended without hesitation.

Both riders were immediately astonished, and at the same time fearful of some ambush or trap. They both quickly unsheathed their swords and looked around for enemies, but none came.

"Who are you?" Dunen quickly asked, keeping the

old man in the corner of his eye even as he searched around for danger.

The man remained calm, although Dunen and Bilob feared the worst.

"I am Nerinee, son of Gorund." he answered.

"Nerinee, the prophet?" Bilob gasped with awe.

The old man nodded.

Dunen was also stunned. One of the great prophets of God now stood before him. He had heard of the prophets of the Lord, but never met one. In times past, they were principal figures amid the great events of Teranda and other cities. History recalled how they called down the power of God on the earth with fire and storm. They were certainly feared and respected by all, including the royal families. But in the recent and peaceful years of Elnoren, they were rarely seen if not even forgotten.

Dunen became very nervous. He knew that for God to send His prophet, meant there was great trouble in the land. Most of all, he feared what the prophet had to say to him. Gathering courage, he moved his horse closer to the prophet.

"I would like to hear what my God has to say to his servant," he told Nerinee.

The man of God was pleased to hear this. He

pointed in the direction they were travelling.

"Not far from here, there is a suitable place to rest. Follow me," he turned and led them on the narrow path.

Dunen and Bilob looked at each other with apprehension. They sheathed their swords and followed. They soon came to an area on the path that was wide enough to tie their horses and for them to sit and rest. The prophet placed himself nearby and waited as they dismounted, tied their horses and retrieved from their bags some food and drink.

They were soon seated on the ground, cross-legged and sharing the food and water. Dunen and Bilob were fairly quiet and actually didn't know how to deal with the prophet. In the middle of their meal, the prophet began to speak.

"Dunen, I am glad to see that our God has spared you from the hands of Ernum. It is with great sorrow that I learned of your father's death. He did much good in the eyes of the Lord, and yet he failed to see the deceitfulness of the evil one and his servants. Lurion serves the dark lord of Dernak. He plans to give Teranda to him, but most of all, he seeks the sword," he said ominously as he looked directly at Dunen.

Dunen already knew this.

"You must stop him before he finds it," he said pointing his bony finger at the young man.

"How can I? I was not trained to lead an army," Dunen questioned him.

"This fault lies with your father, not yours. But it does not matter; it is God's will that you regain the throne," the old man told him.

"How can this be done?" Dunen asked. "The enemy has the city, and who is with me?"

"The Lord will provide. Leave it to Him. In due time, the Lord will bring it to pass, unless you turn away and lose faith," Nerinee warned him.

Dunen felt trapped with his confused emotions. A part of him felt weak and incapable to do anything but at the same time, he wanted revenge against his enemies. He knew much was at stake. This heavy responsibility made him fear, and Nerinee's serious and frowning gaze did not help. Dunen realised that Bilob was looking at him intently, but confidently. It gave him courage to have this mighty man at his side but moreover, that his friend had faith in him.

Nerinee watched him while he reclined a little in his place, and then looked elsewhere as he spoke again.

"You have been taught the story of Dernak's fall into the Devil's way?" Not waiting for an answer, the prophet continued. "It was once a city like Teranda, no different. A people inclined to the Creator - and yet, it was taken in the same way as Teranda. Little by little, the people turned their hearts away, the king forgot his vigilance and in time they yielded to the dark spirits that fell from heaven itself."

"The people of Teranda have not turned their hearts away from God!" Dunen said fervently.

"How sure are you?" he asked Dunen.

Dunen didn't like to consider this question nor wanted to answer it after all that had recently occurred.

"Dernak is now the seat of the evil one, and filled with base people. Day by day they grow in number and further their boundaries. Dernak is now growing in power, more than you know. Teranda has fallen asleep during this time, and now pays dearly for it. You must awaken it, Dunen," Nerinee told him with a commanding voice.

Dunen's felt deeply troubled and overwhelmed by Nerinee's revelations. There seemed to be no other choice for him. Dunen had to put aside his fears and apprehensions and accept the call to regain his father's throne. It would be what his family expected him to do.

"I am the Lord's servant. I will do His will," Dunen told him but felt unsure of himself.

"Nothing more is asked," the prophet answered. "Your father and mother raised you well, but it is regretful that a great debt is left for you to pay. If Teranda is not taken back in the days to come, all of Elnoren will be lost, and no place will be left for us."

Bilob listened wide-eyed and open-mouthed at the ominous words, but he was glad to hear Dunen's decision. Bilob felt a great burden come upon him to help Dunen fulfil the Lord's will and decided he would give his all to the task.

"I must go," Nerinee said and, with this, the prophet stood up.

Dunen and Bilob also quickly got to their feet.

"I am glad to see your obedience. Be very careful, Dunen. The sons of Cain are growing in number and in strength. There is much to do and learn, and much you will see, but be of good courage, the Lord will be your strength. Call on Him when you are troubled and need guidance, He is faithful to answer," the prophet said, laying a hand on the young man's shoulder.

Dunen felt encouraged by the prophet's faith in him and was glad of his wisdom. With that thought, a question came to his mind.

"Nerinee, is my mother alive?" Dunen asked hesitantly, fearing the answer.

"I am sorry. I do not know. It was not revealed to me." He answered compassionately.

Saddened but still hopeful, Dunen nodded understandingly.

"I must now be on my way," Nerinee told them.

"Where are you going? Can we bring you?" asked Dunen, not only wishing to render due courtesy, but feeling strong in his presence.

"I thank you for your generosity, but we have different paths and duties to accomplish. God bless you Dunen. My prayers will be with you. We will see each other again, if God wills," he finally said and with a bow, turned and slowly walked away along the path.

Dunen and Bilob watched him go for a moment. Dunen wished to have spoken more with him, but knew there was little time.

Dunen and Bilob looked at each other and were still amazed at their encounter. Without a word, they silently prepared to continue their journey.

It was not until they reached the valley and night approached that Dunen realised he could have asked the prophet where he could find his army. Surely, he would have known, he thought. Dunen halted his horse and looked back. He then considered the thought of turning back and finding the prophet. But as he considered the possibility, he realised that if the Lord wished him to know the whereabouts, he would have made the prophet tell him. Sadly, he gave up the idea and urged his horse forward.

The day after was the same as the day before. They awoke, ate, and travelled out of the valley and up the other mountain range, on the last leg of their journey.

When night fell, they searched for a dry place to rest. This mountainside was better wooded then the others, and soon they found cover beneath trees with huge canopies and dry ground.

During and after dinner they sat close to the fire, warming themselves from the cool humid night. Dunen had been pensive for much of the day, and Bilob knew enough not to disturb him, but the lack of conversation was bothering him and he wished to talk.

"You have not spoken of your plan to enter the city, Dunen," Bilob carefully broke the silence.

Dunen looked at him and tried to clear his thoughts. "We will approach the northern wall by night and leave the horses in the forest. There is a hidden door along the wall that will open to us and I have the key to it."

With great interest Bilob nodded he understood.

"Forgive me for the lack of conversation, I have much to think of," Dunen added.

"There come such times for all men - and they cannot be avoided it seems," Bilob agreed.

"I fear what Nerinee has revealed to me," Dunen divulged.

"It is troubling, indeed."

"I have many doubts we can regain the city," Dunen said with concern.

"With God, nothing is impossible," Bilob stated confidently.

"True my friend. I forget I am not alone in this battle," Dunen gave him an encouraging smile.

"And we are with you."

Dunen nodded in appreciation and felt some consolation.

"Time to rest. Good night, my friend," Dunen said as he lay down.

"Sleep well."

As Dunen fell asleep, his heart felt a little calmer, glad that the villagers were with him in the struggles to come.

The following day was sunny and hot. Small puddles of mud lay spotted along the path, left behind from the waters that came up from the ground. Not long after, they treaded carefully as they approached the main road to Teranda. Dunen and Bilob looked at each other nervously. Even though the road was narrow and few travelled on it, they still feared any encounter or of unseen eyes. Slowly they approached the road. They listened carefully for any signs of travellers and when they felt that all was clear, they nodded to each other and kicked their horses to a gallop. In a few moments they crossed the road and headed into the forest. Constantly looking behind, they continued their pace for a while and then stopped. They calmed their horses and listened hard for pursuers, but heard nothing.

"All is well," said Bilob.

Dunen nodded with a sigh of relief and then guided his horse into the woods. As they moved along the southern side of the valley, they came to a spot where they could see the city of Teranda.

It rested on a plateau surrounded by a large mountain range. A small valley spread out before it. The city's walls were high and formidable, which never yielded to invaders.

The royal palace lay at the rear of the city and stood slightly higher than the other buildings. The main gate could be seen, with a line of people, animals and carts entering and exiting it, looking like a busy ant trail. A large stretch of cleared land surrounded the city with the exception of a small patch of forest on the southern part.

Dunen had mixed emotions on seeing his beloved city. First he felt sadness for its fall, then anger for those who caused it. He had lived many joyful days within its walls, but now, also his worst memories.

Dunen and Bilob continued their ride through the thick forest. Along the way they crossed the river where Dunen had fished and spent many joyful times. He wondered if those days were gone forever, but deep down he knew his life would never be the same.

At dusk they came to within walking distance of the wall and dismounted their horses. They robed themselves as peasants and hid their swords.

Prepared as best as they could, they sat for a meal and discussed the possible problems they would encounter.

As night came, they waited for a time when the people would be in bed and few would be roaming the streets. They then left their horses behind and walked up the slope towards the wall. They soon came to the edge of the forest, and the darkened wall loomed before them not far away. On the wall, sentinels could be seen keeping their vigil. Immediately, the two cautiously left the forest and silently moved to the wall.

The wall was made of great blocks of stone, sectioned by rounded pillars placed at every hundred paces. Walking along the base of the wall, Dunen stopped before a pillar. He gave a signal to Bilob that this was the secret entrance. In the dim light of the stars, Bilob could see nothing of an entrance, only a wall of stone blocks. For a moment Bilob began to believe Dunen had made a mistake. Dunen then slowly pulled out his shining sword which made Bilob fear it would be seen by the guards on the wall. With his left hand, Dunen began feeling the column and following the joints.

After a long and tense moment, Dunen stopped on a joint. Raising his sword, he then stabbed the column. The sword slid into the joint of the stone blocks up to the hilt. After a few seconds, he withdrew the sword and immediately a low rumble could be heard coming from within the wall. To Bilob's astonishment, he saw the column or, actually, a part of the column the size of a door begin to spin in its place, leaving behind a huge dark entrance. Dunen turned to give a reassuring smile to Bilob, but was met with Bilob's surprised face and gaping mouth. He then disappeared into the dark doorway and Bilob followed hesitantly. They both moved a few paces along the pitch-black tunnel. The low rumble came again, and Bilob saw the entrance close. Bilob then remembered the curves on Dunen's sword and now understood that they made the door open, but how he was not sure. He marvelled at the clever devices of the city folk.

They were now in total darkness once the door closed. Bilob heard Dunen try to start a fire. He saw several sparks light the tunnel briefly, until a light began to grow. It grew large enough to see ten paces or so within the tunnel. Dunen raised the light and began seeking along the wall. Finding a torch attached to the wall, he lit the torch with his fire and then extinguished the original flame.

Dunen noticed Bilob looking all around with great

curiosity. "What are you looking for?" he asked.

"Where is the one who opened the door?" he asked bewildered.

"No man has opened the door for us," he answered flatly.

"Was it an angel?" he asked becoming fearful.

"No!" he answered annoyingly, "I will explain some other time."

Bilob nodded but still looked around with fear.

"Truly, your people have done great work with stone and metal," Bilob told him.

"This is true," Dunen agreed being also impressed of the builders skills. "The other door will bring us into an alley connected to a road within the city."

Dunen moved ahead and came to the end of the tunnel. Bilob could now see the other door which Dunen spoke of.

"Are you ready, my friend?" Dunen asked, poised at the wall.

"Yes," answered Bilob as he joined him.

Dunen placed his hood up over his head, and his face was now a shadow. Once again he slipped his sword into a crack in the wall and the door soon turned creating an opening. The two men stepped out into an alley and the night sky welcomed them. A moment after, the door closed by itself.

Bilob looked back with awe. He and his people had heard of the ingenuity of the city dwellers, but this surpassed the stories told.

Dunen motioned with his hand for Bilob to follow. Moving to the corner of the alley, he peered out into the street. Seeing nobody in sight, he stepped out. They were now both out in the street. It was fairly quiet. No lights shone within the homes, and the street was deserted. They quickly began to walk down roads and alleys and stopped twice to hide from people walking by. Bilob was agitated and constantly looked around for trouble. He did not feel comfortable in the city, being a man of the woods, and kept looking everywhere anxiously. After a long brisk walk, they stopped in the middle of the street, facing a house. Dunen pointed to the partly wooden and brick house.

"This is a friend," he then looked around verifying, that no one was around. He began to whistle a short call to the house, towards the upper rooms. Dunen waited for a response. Receiving none, he repeated the tune again. This time a light appeared inside one of the rooms. In the shadows of the room, someone came to the window and moved the curtains to look down into the street. The person left the window and Dunen moved to the door of the house. After a short wait, they could hear someone come to the door, unlock it, and open the door slightly.

Dunen and Bilob quickly moved inside. The door was shut behind them, and an old man stood before them. He was in his night robe, and a lantern was in his hand. He was an elderly man with refined features and delicate skin. His soft wrinkled face and piercing eyes spoke of a man of great learning. He was surprised and a little worried by the midnight call.

"Who are you, and how do you know of the call?" The old man looked at them intently, not recognising the hooded Dunen or his large companion.

"Keren, it is I, Dunen." Dunen uncovered his head. The old man gasped with astonishment, and backed away with shock. He then fell to one knee and bowed.

"Master! Oh! My beloved master!" As he raised his head, the old man's surprise turned to great joy, and tears began to fill his eyes. "By God's holy mercy, you live! Oh, thanks be to God, who has not forsaken His people. You live!"

"Yes, my friend. Come, we must speak, and we do not have much time."

Keren raised himself and led them into the dining room.

"Oh, what great joy to see you alive and well?"

"I am also happy to see you, my dear friend," Dunen said and turning to Bilob, he told him, "He is an old friend of my father's, and once a counsellor of the throne."

"Please sit down Master and rest."

Dunen and Bilob sat down at the table.

Fear suddenly came over Keren's face. "What are you doing here? You are in great danger in the city!" he said anxiously. "You must leave at once! Have you gone mad?"

"You see? He too believes this was madness!" exclaimed Bilob with a disappointing smirk.

"I had no choice! We were careful not to be seen."

"Your pardon, master, but this was not a wise decision. Oh, no! Not wise at all," Keren said firmly and with great dissatisfaction.

"We are of the same mind. You and I," Bilob said as he pointed to each other.

Dunen gave him an unpleasant glare.

"There is no time to argue, we are here."

"Yes, of course. Forgive me."

"Keren! I need to know," Dunen asked with apprehension. "Is my mother alive?"

"Yes, my lord. She lives!. She escaped the same day as you. Menfre, Danar, Shadly and Manru survived as well. They fought a great fight and escaped," Keren told him excitedly.

Dunen almost broke into tears, as joy filled his heart and great relief came over him. These words he had dreaded to ask for so long now brought a great flood of peace and joy. He felt a great burden had suddenly come off him.

"Blessed be to God! Thank you my God."

Bilob also was happy over the good news, and happy his friend was comforted.

Keren nodded happily. "Are you thirsty my lord?" Not waiting for an answer he scurried away into the kitchen and soon returned with a jug of juice and three cups.

"It was a terrible day, indeed. When I heard of your father and brother-" Keren stopped, unwilling to remember the heart breaking event.

"Yes, I know. I saw their last moments," Dunen told him as he drank.

"You saw? You were there? Dreadful!" he said solemnly and grieved to hear this. "Oh, how foolish we were to be ignorant of the evil workings in our midst. Who would have guessed that Ernum, from his kingdom far away, could conceive to stretch out his arm over Teranda? We have become careless in our peace, and now we have been brought low."

"Indeed, we have paid a great price and now we must open our eyes and correct our error," Dunen said gravely. "As long as Ernum is alive, there will be no peace for us nor would it linger if we had it."

"Yes, we must do something," Keren agreed. "And yet, the army was reduced to half its size, and Lurion holds the city. What can we do now?"

"Half our strength!" Dunen repeated the words with shock and dismay. With those numbers, Dunen believed it impossible to take back the city.

"There must be a way, Keren," Dunen wondered after what Nerinee had told him.

Keren considered his master's words and nodded with agreement. "Only the Lord knows," he then gazed at Dunen, judging him a moment. "You have changed, Dunen. No more the young man I knew. I believe the Creator has much work for you to do."

Dunen nodded reluctantly.

"Do you know where my mother is?" Dunen asked.

"She must by now be with the army," Keren reported.

"Do you know where?"

"Oh, no. The location of the army is kept secret, but I would wager they would be found in the woods of Forwilda."

"Yes, I agree. I must find them," he said as he got to his feet, anxious to start his search.

"Be careful, master. We cannot be sure if Lurion knows the place and waits for you go there! All the roads are watched."

"True. But I must join them. I will be careful. We must be on our way."

They all moved towards the door.

"Yes, master. Would you need anything for the journey?"

"No, thank you my friend."

"Very well. My liege, once again I say what great joy I have to see you alive and well."

Dunen laid his hand on Keren's shoulder. "Farewell, my friend. The Lord willing, we will see each other again, face to face. Be careful. If they seek your life, flee and take others with you."

"Yes, of course. The Lord keep you and your friend," Keren said and bowed.

"I thank you as well, Keren," Bilob said with a bow.

Dunen put on his hood. Keren opened the door and looked out. Sure that all was safe, he motioned the way was clear. Dunen and Bilob stepped out into the deserted street and began their brisk walk back.

Keren watched them go, and then closed the door. Troubled for his master, he quickly sought God in prayer for his safety.

As fast as they dared, the two retraced their course, and were soon not far from the secret entrance. Suddenly footsteps caught their attention. They quickly searched for a place to hide. Finding a small alley not far away, they hid themselves in the dark. After a few moments had passed, a group of soldiers appeared around the corner. Their armor clanked and their loud talk broke the silence as they marched. They passed the alley where Dunen and Bilob were hiding and continued down the street, turning the corner into another street.

Dunen and Bilob breathed a sigh of relief. Cautiously they looked into the street and left their hiding place. Just as they came to the next corner, a soldier, walking briskly, came around the corner and almost crashed into them.

"Halt!" he said quickly, drawing his sword when he saw them.

Dunen and Bilob froze before him.

"Who are you, and what is your business?" the soldier said roughly, as he noticed Bilob's size. "It is forbidden to walk the streets at this time."

Dunen and Bilob's minds raced to give an answer.

"Ah, we have come late from a friend and now are returning home," Bilob answered.

The soldier was now suspicious, especially since Dunen's face was barely visible beneath his hood. For a moment he examined them both, and then turned to Dunen. "You! Show your face," he commanded, pointing with his sword.

Both men looked at each other a moment, not sure what to do. In a flash, Bilob grabbed the soldier's arm carrying the sword with his right hand and struck a mighty blow straight on the soldier's chin with his left. The force of the blow sent the soldier backward across the street, crashing into the wall of a house. The limp body then crumbled down to the ground with a great clatter. There he lay, motionless.

"You could have done this in a more silent manner," Dunen told him, slightly agitated.

"Forgive me," Bilob could only answer.

Far down the street, the other soldiers, hearing the noise and missing their comrade, were rapidly approaching.

"Let us hurry," Dunen urged him.

They both began to run. Moments later, warning whistles blared from where they had left the unconscious soldier. Dunen knew the city was alerted and other guards would soon come into the area. He and Bilob continued their pace until they came to the street that led to the tunnel. Stopping at the corner, Dunen looked carefully down the street, and saw to his great dismay five soldiers marching briskly in their direction, their swords in hand.

"Soldiers block the way, five of them. We have no choice but to fight them. There is no time to go around them," Dunen told Bilob urgently.

Bilob did not like the idea, but reluctantly agreed with a nod. The alarm spread throughout the city and it began to get noisier with activity by the second. Many more soldiers would be called to the troubled spot, and they would soon be trapped and outnumbered.

Unsheathing their swords, they waited for the approaching soldiers to draw closer. When Dunen gave the signal, they jumped into the street and rushed the surprised soldiers. Bilob engaged three soldiers and Dunen the other two. The soldiers retreated a few steps at first, surprised by the onslaught, but then stood their ground. The clanging of swords and shouts filled the street, but not a house opened a light to view the conflict, only peering eyes watched the confrontation.

With a swipe of his sword, Bilob dispatched one soldier who dared try to stab him. Dunen in turn allowed one soldier an open area to strike, which he took, only to realize too late that Dunen was waiting for him with a thrust of his sword, leaving him only one opponent. At about the same moment, Bilob was able to slay another of his opponents. When that was done, Bilob's last adversary, standing before this dark menacing giant, decided not to fight him alone, and took the occasion to escape down the street. At the same moment, Dunen cut down his remaining adversary.

"Quickly, my lord. Others approach," said Bilob anxiously.

Dunen was surprised for a moment to hear Bilob call him by his title. He immediately led the way. They soon entered the alley that led to the secret door. Dunen found the crack after a long and nervous moment of difficulty in the dark. He stabbed the wall with his sword, and they were soon inside the secret tunnel. Without stopping, Dunen ran to the other end and again inserted his sword into the secret slot.

"Turn out the light," he told Bilob as the door began to open. Bilob took the torch off the wall extinguished the fire. They were soon outside the city wall and running into the forest. Without stopping, they ran through the dark forest until they found their horses. Quickly they mounted and sped off.

#

Within the city of Teranda, a captain of the guard nervously paced the marble floor of a waiting chamber in the palace. From one of two doors, Rondree, dressed in evening robe, entered the quarters, displeased by the night call. The captain came to attention and bowed.

"What is it?" Rondree asked.

"Sire. A peculiar confrontation occurred along the southern wall, which I must report."

"Go on," said Rondree, knowing his men would not dare awaken him for minor trouble.

"Two men have engaged six of our soldiers and killed four. One was able to report the incident, but no trace could be found of the assailants."

"You awakened me for a rebel skirmish?" Rondree said angrily.

"No sire, but one fought as a nobleman and was

hooded. The other was a villager. A giant of a man."

Rondree's anger subsided as the soldier's report intrigued him. Slowly he paced the room as he considered the recent event. The captain watched and waited nervously.

"Was there anything else peculiar about the two men?" asked Rondree, stopping near the captain. The captain began to think.

"Nothing else."

"What was a villager doing inside the city?" Rondree asked, speaking to himself. The soldier, overhearing his question also wondered.

"Truly this is odd. I can assure you, sire, that no outsiders have come through the gates, as you ordered," the soldier explained, fearing to being blamed.

Rondree gave him a questionable look and then returned to his thoughts. After a long moment, Rondree turned to the captain.

"Villagers do not like linger in the city, especially at night. I want you to send spies to search the villages in the valley of Soloneb. This must be done at once, captain."

"Yes sire."

"If any sign of Dunen is found by the spies, you

will advise me immediately," Rondree commanded.

"It will be done as you command," the captain quickly bowed and left the room.

Rondree was now concerned. If Dunen found refuge with the villagers of Soloneb, it would make it difficult to find and kill him. And what he feared the most was the involvement of the villagers in his affairs. If they would enter the conflict, the villagers could pose a serious problem to their plans. Disturbed at the thought, Rondree tightened his robe with determination and returned to his room.

Chapter 6
DARK VISITORS

After riding through most of the night, Dunen and Bilob settled just before dawn in the northern mountains overlooking Teranda. They both went to sleep and woke up late in the morning. They were slightly bruised from the recent struggle, and had to take care of some minor cuts. During breakfast they spoke concerning what to do next.

"I must go and try to find my mother and my father's army," Dunen told Bilob.

"I understand my friend," Bilob agreed with some concern.

"I must join my father's army. I am sure they seek for me. They must all wonder where I am and if I live," Dunen replied as he considered what his mother must be thinking.

"I will go with you."

"You have done more than was required. You need not come."

"I wish it. I promised to help you," Bilob said with determination.

"Very well, then." Dunen could only say over Bilob's stern gaze. "I hoped you would come", he then added.

Bilob was happy to hear it.

"The forest of Forwilda is over a day's journey."

"Forwilda! Those are dark woods I hear, and hard to roam within," Bilob said with concern.

"Yes, but -" Dunen was interrupted by the snapping of a twig close by and just behind them.

In a instant, both jumped to their feet with swords in hand. From between some bushes a few feet away, Nerinee the prophet stood watching them.

"Nerinee!" blurted Dunen as he expelled a great sigh of relief.

"It is I," he said as he approached them. "Your blades prove unwelcoming," he said while staring at their weapons.

They had both forgotten their drawn swords and menacing postures, being surprised by his appearance. They slowly relaxed and put their swords away.

Bilob and Dunen bowed respectfully before him.

"I am glad to see you again," said Dunen.

"Your venture into the city went well I see," Nerinee stated calmly, but saw their bandaged arms.

"Fairly well."

"We encountered a little trouble," Bilob added with a smirk.

"Hmm," Nerinee articulated with a slight displeasure and then sat on the ground. "What have you learned, my lord?"

"I have been told my mother lives, and that half of my father's army are gathered in a secret place. Bilob and I go now to search for them," Dunen answered happily.

"It is good news, but you will not join your mother," Nerinee said flatly.

Dunen and Bilob were stunned at Nerinee's words.

"What!" Dunen exclaimed.

"You will return to Maarkaat," the old man told Dunen.

"I do not understand! My place is beside my mother and with my father's army, yet you wish me to go to Maarkaat! For what purpose?" Dunen demanded, flustered.

"Your decision is what any man would do, but the Lord's will is different," Nerinee said, undisturbed by Dunen's reaction.

Nerinee's words brought Dunen to his senses. He did not like what he heard, having the desire to see his mother, and yet, if the message was from God, he knew he should heed the counsel and obey it. After struggling a moment with himself, he said with some frustration, "Very well. I will obey the

107

word of the Lord. Forgive me for my outburst," he said reluctantly.

Nerinee smiled, happy to hear Dunen submit to God. "A good decision. Trust in the Lord and He will not fail you."

"Can I be told why I must go to Maarkaat?"

"That, God did not reveal unto me. You will know when you reach Maarkaat, I presume."

"How long must I remain there?" Dunen asked with some anxiety.

"This neither do I know," Nerinee replied.

"You wish me to go to Maarkaat without knowing why, and you wish for me to stay there without knowing how long, when great trouble is afoot? You ask much," Dunen said frustratingly.

"I ask nothing. I am a messenger of the living God," he said, his voice growing deeper, "He will reveal His will to you in due time. The hand of God is working in the affairs of men. You must allow Him to lead you," Nerinee told him as he got up and faced Dunen.

He gave Dunen a long piercing stare that made Dunen forget his complaints. Once again he forgot that more important matters were at stake than his personal desires. Greater things were at work, which he knew not, and wondered when they would be revealed to him. He knew he must listen to the counsel of the prophet, and pray God for guidance as well.

"Very well. I will return to Maarkaat."

Nerinee seemed relieved, and changed his mood.

"You will be careful not to take the road, and you will return the way you came," he advised.

Dunen wished to take the open road and arrive at Maarkaat quickly, but he agreed with Nerinee that it would be safer to go by the back ways.

"We will do as you say."

Bilob was happy to hear that they were returning to Maarkaat.

Nerinee once again gave Dunen a serious look, "Understand, Dunen, you must now be careful. What you say and do must be proceeded by much prayer and guidance. To stray by your own reasoning could bring much harm upon yourself and others."

Dunen nodded, assuring him.

"Much is at stake and the evil one has made great inroads," the old man reminded him, "He must be defeated!"

"I am grateful for your counsel."

"I will see you again, when the time is needful."

The conversation ended and Nerinee departed

from them, walking off down the path. After watching him go, they immediately packed their possessions and continued their journey. Dunen was silent and kept to himself. Bilob on the other hand, was excited about what he had heard and could not wait to tell his family and friends.

After an uneventful trip across the mountains, Dunen and Bilob joined the main road that led to Maarkaat. About mid-afternoon, the two travellers arrived at the village. Friends and Bilob's family hurriedly came to welcome them back with much joy and relief. Marani also was there, and was glad to see her brother home and to see that Dunen had returned. Celkob soon came along, and praised God for their safe return. He quickly urged them to enter his house and allowed others to come in and hear about their journey.

Celkob sat in his place, with Dunen and Bilob beside him. Other villagers, including Marani, sat in a circle or remained standing along the walls as they waited impatiently for Dunen to begin.

"Tell us now of your journey," Celkob asked.

Dunen began to relate the events that took place in the city, about their narrow escape and their meeting with the prophet Nerinee. At the mention of the prophet, the villagers gasped with awe and began speaking in whispers amongst themselves excitedly. Celkob was also surprised, and it seemed to Dunen that the news had made him grim and troubled.

"I was told by Nerinee that the Lord wanted me to return here – the reason I know not," Dunen finished and anxiously waited for Celkob's thoughts.

For a long moment Celkob stared at the floor. Then he spoke in a solemn voice, "A prophet!" he said and then looked at Dunen and the others as if wondering if he should reveal his thoughts. "They appear only when the time is dire and the fate of many is at stake."

They all looked at each with troubled stares.

"We must be very careful of our decisions, and we must trust our God to help us," said Celkob. "Our Creator does not send His prophets about lightly. Much prayer is needed for Dunen and his people."

All in the room agreed as a somber mood fell over the villagers.

"I am glad to hear your mother is alive," Celkob added.

"So am I, but she does not know that I live," Dunen said frustratingly.

"I grieve with you also my friend, but do what is asked of you. Trust in our God," Celkob exhorted.

Dunen nodded, but still found it hard to accept.

"You must be tired from the long ride. Go, eat and rest; tomorrow we will further speak of these matters, "Celkob urged.

"That agrees with me," Bilob said, relishing the thought of a hot supper from his mother's stove.

Dunen grinned at his friend's great appetite.

"I am in need of some rest," Dunen agreed.

"You will come tomorrow, at the early light. We have much to discuss," Celkob told him.

"I will come," Dunen assured him.

They all got up and left Celkob's tent. Villagers surrounded Bilob, wanting to hear more details of his journey to Teranda. Dunen followed behind, but his heart was elsewhere. He wondered how God would clearly show him what to do? He didn't want to make a mistake, nor disappoint his family and friends.

As the sun went down in Maarkaat, Dunen lay on his bed, after enjoying a swim in the river and a good meal. As he looked up at the dark ceiling, he started to think about the recent events and what Nerinee had told him. Ernum's reason to take

Teranda was not only to conquer the region of Elnoren, but mainly to get the sword of Teranda. With it, Ernum would gain an even greater advantage against his foes. In battle, his enemies would tremble before him and evil men would be emboldened to join him. His next step would be to conquer the port city of Sandinor. Then all the great cities would be his and who no one would dare go against him. As he considered these things, Dunen trembled with fear over the gravity of the situation. These gentle and kind villagers of Soloneb, who have become good friends, would also be attacked and subdued sooner or later by Ernum. They would all suffer the more for having sheltered him. Dunen grew angry at the thought, which made him the more resolute to regain Teranda at all cost. Hopefully, before Ernum could find the sword.

Slowly, his tired body pulled him away from his disturbed reflections and sent him into a deep slumber.

#

Not far from the village of Maarkaat, four dark figures moved quietly and cautiously through the forest. Wearing dark clothes with faces and hands blackened, they could barely be seen in the night.

Each one carried a black scabbard and sword on his back, while only one toted a short bow. Completely shrouded in black, they blended into the shadows. With controlled ease and care, they glided through the forest hardly making any noise. Every obstacle that offered a place to hide was used. Like cats stalking for a kill, they continued to move forward through the woods.

Not far from their position, a Maarkaat sentinel watched the dark forest from his camouflaged perch in a tree. Carefully, his trained eyes and ears surveyed the grounds below, but he was incapable of detecting the invisible enemies.

One of the dark figures, as he looked up at the trees, spotted the hidden post and quickly signalled the others. They stopped and became as stone. The archer left the others to position himself further away. As the three continued, the bowman searched for an opening in the sentinel's position. Once he could clearly see the villager, he cocked an arrow and let loose.

Not a moment passed before a cry was heard, and the villager fell through the branches and crashed to the ground.

The bowman quickly ran to examine the dead villager. Satisfied with his victim's death, he left to join his companions. With a faster pace, the four went through the woods until the lights of Maarkaat could be seen. Hiding behind trees, they scrutinized the village. At this time of night, only a few villagers walked the grounds. Conversations could be heard from the houses.

The four left their place and began to follow the length of the village, carefully keeping an eye out as to not be seen. At one end of the village, one of the stables that housed the horses of the village was set apart in a large clearing. Over thirty horses were kept in stalls in this one area.

The four figures crawled over to the stalls. Some horses whimpered at the unknown men. Exchanging instructions for a moment, the four then separated, each going to a group of stalls. One by one they examined the horses, until one of the men called to the others. They gathered around the one who had called, and he pointed to the horse's saddle. The saddle bore the emblems of a lion, and the markings of Teranda's cavalry.

With a nod, the strangers then left the stables and moved toward the village homes.

Cries filled his head, as Dunen began to wake up. Still groggy, he thought it was just a dream, until the screams grew louder and clearer. Suddenly he knew they were real. Raising himself off his bed, he listened to the shouts in the village. Something was wrong, and he guessed by the voices that there was fighting. Quickly he searched for his scabbard in the dark room and unsheathed his sword. Wasting no time, he crashed through the doors and stopped. Dunen could see men leaving their homes and racing to the village square. Just as he was about to go himself, someone shouted his name. "Dunen!"

Whirling around in the direction of the call, Dunen saw a dark object move quickly toward him. For a second, he could not distinguish the form. But as it came closer, the village lights made out the shape of a human form and bearing a black pointed object, a sword. Just in time, he readied his sword and blocked a blow that sent him reeling backwards. The black assailant came on without a pause. Dunen regained his footing as he blocked the deadly blows. His adversary's swordsmanship quickly told him that he was fighting a soldier of the city, worse yet, a Targot. Dunen doubled his efforts to stay alive. Finding it difficult to follow the black blade as it disappeared against the night, Dunen could only use his experience to guess the swordsman's next thrust.

The Targot's onslaught was fierce and unrelenting. Dunen feared he would be tired soon and had little chance of planning a counterattack.

Suddenly, the Targot jerked several times and uttered a cry of pain. Dropping his sword, he then fell to the ground, with several arrows piercing his back.

Dunen looked up and saw, not far away, two villagers with bows in hand. Bilob came running through the homes toward Dunen, his great sword in hand.

"Dunen, are you well?" The big friend asked as he stopped before the dead Targot.

"Yes," Dunen answered as he gasped for air from the struggle.

"By the living fathers! Who are these?" Bilob asked while the bowmen joined them.

"These? How many were they?" Dunen asked with concern.

"We are not sure. Some say there were two and others five. Whatever their number only this one remains," Bilob declared.

"These are called Targots!" Dunen blurted, at once concerned and disgusted.

The villagers exchanged glances with great interest.

Celkob and a dozen village men came striding to their side.

"Dunen!" Celkob called out.

"Here, my friend. I am well," he assured him.

Celkob was relieved to see him, and joined the others as they looked on the Targot.

"Who are they?" Celkob asked.

"Targots," Dunen answered. "Spies of Ernum, well trained to search and kill," he explained. "They came for me."

"And they found you," Celkob added.

"But they failed," Bilob proclaimed proudly.

"If not for your men, I would be dead," Dunen told them.

Celkob nodded. "We have lost four of our men, and two are seriously injured."

Dunen was upset over the loss.

"They were swift," a villager could only say.

"Lurion will know that I am here," Dunen said with dread. "He will now send his army and your village will be destroyed. I should not have stayed, and now some are dead because of it!"

"Dunen! We all share this trouble," Celkob asserted.

"They are also our enemies," Bilob confirmed with clenched fists.

"But what are you against their numbers? I must join my father's army. They must know that I am alive."

"And go against Nerinee's counsel?" Celkob reminded him.

Dunen clenched his fist and grew frustrated. "What is the point of my being here? Is it to bring destruction to the innocent?" he exclaimed, pointing to the village and the unseen dead.

"Dunen, I believe the Lord has sent you to us for good reason. You need our help," Celkob answered calmly.

Dunen's dilemma subsided, for he was unsure what Celkob meant. How could a small village help him against an army of trained and well equipped warriors?

"Patience, my friend. Let the Lord do His work. You will soon see your purpose here," Celkob exhorted.

Dunen stared at him for a moment and then nodded reluctantly, feeling guilty nonetheless and unhappy with the lost lives.

Chapter 7
CORDS OF WAR

The evening after the attack, during a clear night sky, the stars shone brightly over a large square-clearing deep in the northern woods of the Soloneb valley. All along the rim of a large field, torches lit the grounds. Several dozen villagers stood about, some speaking to one another in groups and others moving from one group to another. All of them were well armed with swords and bows strapped to their backs. Not far from them, horses were tied together. In the centre of the clearing, more torches lighted a circular stone structure. Seven huge stone walls rose ten feet above the ground. They were separated by high openings. No roof covered the structure; it remained open to the sky. From afar, the pillars seemed like seven gigantic chairs placed in a circle, and in some ways they were.

Inside, at the bottom of each of the pillars, an elder villager sat on a stone block, except for one. The floor was made of bricks that converged toward the centre like a large target. Villagers were spoke with one another and to those who were seated around them. In one of the chairs, Celkob was seated, while Bilob stood next to him. Celkob raised his head to look up at Bilob and said, "How is your sister, Bilob?"

Bilob, who was looking around with interest at the other villagers, snapped his attention to Celkob. "Marani? She is well. Why do you ask?" he said curiously.

"I believe her heart beats for Dunen," Celkob replied.

Bilob disappointingly agreed with a nod and a grunt.

"I hope she will have what she seeks," Celkob said.

"I am fond of Dunen, but he is a man of the city, and she a women of the land," Bilob pointed out. "What have they in common? He will seek for one of his own kind."

"True. I am concerned for her."

Some commotion came to their attention from outside, as another group of villagers approached. They all turned to look outside the wall and see the new arrivals. From within the dark forest, a light could be seen drawing closer. Soon a group of five villagers entered the clearing, with one holding a flaming torch as he led the way. The third horseman was covered with a light blue mantle with bronze stripes streaming across. His hair was white with age, but he conveyed himself with strength and assurance.

They led their horses to one side of the clearing and dismounted. The leader entered the circular structure with a calm and graceful walk as others bowed. Immediately, the aides left the elders alone in the stone structure. The newcomer entered the circle slowly, looked around to all those who were seated. After he acknowledged their presence, he then walked over to the empty seat. The moment he stood before his seat, all became silent. After a short time of reflection, the elder raised his head, looking slightly above the pillars into the sky and began to speak with a strong but majestic voice.

"Long ago, in our early beginnings, when strife filled our hearts and blood was shed amongst us, being the sons of Cain, the God of mercy manifested Himself and brought us peace. He gathered us from darkness and brought us to His marvellous light. We then covenanted to be one, brothers bound together in the same faith before the Creator. And so we have done according to His will."

Looking to the elders, the newcomer continued, "Gathered at a call from the heart of one, we come to share the need. Who has called this most solemn assembly?" With these last words, he sat down.

A moment passed and Celkob rose from his chair. All the elders turned to give their attention to him.

"Once again the promises made long ago are kept by faithful men who love and obey our God and his commandments," Celkob acknowledged.

"What is it my brother?" the elder asked.

Celkob moved to the centre. His thoughts were now concentrated on the words he would say. "It is true that once we were a people of strife and warred against each other, but for many years now we are at peace. So also we must remember who brought us this peace." The name of Anandun was whispered by many. "Anandun was cherished by our fathers, for he brought forth the word that has bound us till this day. He was a son of Seth, and built the city of Teranda," all nodded in agreement. "We owe much to him and now, I believe, comes the time to repay our debt."

A deep silence again came over the circle.

"You have heard that his son, King Favro was killed, as well as his son Tharan, by one named Lurion, not many days ago. The king's youngest son Dunen, by God's grace, was spared and has found refuge in my village."

At his last words, the silence broke with a great chatter of interest from all the men from within and even those who listen outside.

"By God's hand, Dunen was found by one of my people, barely alive. I believe he was given to us that we may have occasion to repay the great kindness done to us?" Celkob asked.

After a short consideration, many elders nodded in agreement.

"Although these are the affairs of city dwellers, these recent events concern us all," he went on. "Lurion is a puppet of Ernum, king of Dernak. The words that come from afar are true. He is a son of Cain and despises the children of the Lord. His wicked ways are well known to all and do not have to be spoken. Although his kingdom is far away, his hands have now reached our peaceful lands. Last night, spies of Ernum entered our village and killed four of my people and injured others. They sought for the life of Dunen."

For a moment, not a soul spoke as they were shocked by the news, then all erupted into many angered conversations. This continued until the chief elder rose to calm them. Slowly they quieted down and gave again Celkob their attention.

"They now know that Dunen is among us and will certainly come for him with great force. I and my people have decided to help him."

Bilob grinned proudly at Celkob's words and decision.

"I have come to seek those who will join us to repay this debt in this great time of need. We must save the life of Dunen from them who wish to destroy him, and help him regain the throne of his father and grandfather Anandun. To do otherwise, I give you my warning, will bring evil days upon us all, and none of us will escape," Celkob said, and then withdrew a small dagger from his belt and dropped it at the center of the stone floor.

Calmly he bowed and returned to his seat. The elders began to contemplate and discuss the matter with one another. After some time, one by one, the elders withdrew a small dagger from their belts and cast them within the circle. Celkob bowed his head with relief and thanksgiving to the Lord for their commitment to join his effort.

Chapter 8
THE CALL

Late afternoon, amidst the camp of the Terandian army, a rider swiftly galloped across to the pavilions. Quickly halting his horse, he dismounted and entered the tent of command.

Inside, Menfre and Manru were busy going about their duties and discussing the state of the army. The messenger quickly entered and bowed.

Menfre noticed the messenger's anxious expression and commanded, "Speak."

The messenger began, slightly out of breath. "My captain, word has come that Lurion is moving his army."

Menfre and Manru looked at each other gravely and realised that the time had come.

"What is their destination?" asked Menfre.

"We know not my lord, but they travel the King's road towards the north."

Quickly they raised themselves and looked on the great map that displayed the regions of Elnoren, Sousenden and a part of the northern region as well as the great sea to the east. Teranda was at the centre of the map. The etchings of a sword and shield in the woods of Forwilda far south of

Teranda marked their army's present position.

"North. To the north we have Karlun, Ener and further the villages of Soloneb," Menfre said.

"Karlun and Ener have already succumbed," Manru informed them.

"This leaves us the tribesmen."

They stared at each other as the same thought crossed their mind.

"We must warn Shadly and Lady Elena," Manru said.

"Indeed." Turning to a porter Menfre commanded to have them fetched. He then asked the messenger, "How many are there?"

"A third."

"This is good news," said Menfre with great relief.

"If we plan to attack the remaining force, we will still be outnumbered," Manru added quickly.

"Yes, but with a greater chance of success."

"True."

The door coverings were moved aside as Shadly and Elena entered.

"My Lady, we have news that Lurion is moving a third of his army to the north," Menfre reported.

Elena calmly moved over to the table and looked over the map. They all waited as she considered the news.

"What do you believe is the reason?" she asked Menfre.

"We are not so sure, my lady," turning to the messenger. "Have you any knowledge of the reason?"

"The reason is not known, my lord."

"Which force is being used?" asked Shadly.

"Horseman."

"They wish to travel quickly," added Danar, "to strike quickly and return quickly. A wise move."

"This could be a lure for us to come out of our hiding," Shadly said, "thinking we will attack their main army and then attack us from behind."

"This I doubt. They will gain nothing from this," Menfre believed.

"Then for what other reason?" Manru asked.

"Is it possible they have found Dunen?" Elena asked with concern.

The captains looked at each other and considered the suggestion.

"If Dunen found refuge with the villagers of Soloneb," Menfre added, "they do well to send a large force. These villagers are not to be taken lightly."

"We cannot be sure of this?" reminded Shadly.

"Whatever the reason, we have an important

decision to make. If we go now and it truly is a trap, we forfeit the army and lose our hope of regaining Teranda. If they seek for Dunen, and we do not come to his aid, we send him to his death," explained Manru.

"And we have little time to decide," Menfre added solemnly.

Troubled by the difficult situation, they looked at one another with indecision and at the large map. Elena worried for Dunen, wished to act, but at the same time, she did not wish to destroy their only hope of saving Teranda.

"Menfre, what must we do?" she asked nervously.

Shadly answered instead, "We are better to wait and see Lurion's plan unfold than foolishly take a grave risk."

"But if they seek for Dunen and kill him, what hope have we? We must move and pray that God be with us. If we delay but one day, they will be able to kill him and turn to fight us with their full strength," Manru said looking to both Elena and Menfre.

Elena turned her hard gaze to Menfre, who stared at the map while deeply considering the difficult situation.

"Menfre, you must decide. You have fought with

my husband many battles and know his mind in these matters. I cannot give my say, my heart is troubled and my thoughts unsure," Elena said to Menfre, resigning herself from the critical decision.

Menfre expected this decision to be his to make and the weight of it was heavy.

"I must have a time to consider all that I have heard," Menfre said gravely.

"Very well," Elena agreed as Menfre gave a slight bow and left the tent.

They all looked at him go and felt the great burden that lay on him.

Outside, night had fully come. Menfre looked around and then walked off towards the forest that encircled the huge army. A long walk brought him outside the perimeter of the camp. Waving to a sentinel to warn of his purpose, he entered the forest. The dark woods surrounded him with their tall ominous trees. Menfre felt lighter being outside and away from the camp. He kept himself from thinking of his decision till he was further off in the forest all alone. Moving as best as he could amid the trees, he found a fallen tree on which he stopped and sat. Looking up, a few stars pierced through the tree canopy and twinkled against the black sky.

"Oh! God, creator of all things. I carry a great burden. A grave decision is laid upon me. I must confess a burden too great for me. I beg your help. What am I to do? Have mercy and help me. What must I do? The life of my king lies in my hands! Your people look to me for an answer that I am unsure to give."

For a moment Menfre looked up into the trees as if waiting to hear a voice and yet none came. His heart felt the more troubled. Time was short and too important to let pass. Feeling feeble by the weight of responsibility, he slowly slid from the trunk to fall on his knees and bowed himself to the ground. "Oh, God, comfort your servant. Give me your peace and wisdom. Must we go, your people, or refrain? For I believe we must save my prince. But what is your will?"

As he anguished over the question, he sensed a growing peace. "If we go, will you be with us?" Again Menfre sensed a peace that encouraged him. His doubts gradually began to disappear as he considered sending the army. The more he contemplated his decision, the more he felt assured of his decision and hoped it was God's will. Gladness replaced his sorrow and tears of joy came to his eyes. After a time of praise to his caring God, Menfre forced himself to return to camp and give the word.

All along the way he gladly praised the God of all creation. Leaving the forest, the sentinel was much surprised to see his captain happy, when not long ago his face was filled with gloom. The soldier himself was encouraged by his great smile and it filled him with joy and strength after so many long days of uncertainty.

"The Lord be with you captain, my captain," he said proudly.

"And the Lord with you my brother," he said as he raised his hand at him and hurriedly pressed on to the camp.

Not far from the pavilions, Menfre recognised an officer of one of the battalions.

"Suriat!" he called.

The officer surprised by the call, mainly because of its vibrant tone, quickly came to him.

"Yes, my captain."

"Gather the officers in my tent immediately, and give word we march early morning."

The officer's eyes widened with concern, but on seeing the confident expression of his captain, he also felt assured.

"Yes, my captain, immediately!" With a quick bow he sprinted off.

Menfre continued his trek to the main tent and burst into the room. Manru and Shadly were slouched in their chairs and slowly turned to look at who entered so boldly. They knew immediately by Menfre's appearance that he had come to a decision. This made them straighten themselves in their chairs.

"What of it, Menfre?" asked Manru anxiously.

"We march."

Manru grinned with excitement. "Good, and surely the Lord be with us."

Shadly was not so confident.

"I pray you are right or we shall play our last part on this earth."

Menfre and Manru nodded worryingly.

Chapter 9
SPOILED DINNER

Lurion relished his baked lamb and chewed on it with great zest. Two of his counsellors ate with him at the table and watched him warily. The dining hall was silent except for the noises made by their eating. Guards stood watch on both sides of the great hall doors. The palace dining room had seen many kings come into power and royal descendants, but not a dictator. Lurion seemed happy and thoughtful as he ate. Not long after cleaning a lamb's leg and laying the bone in his plate, he reached for a glass of wine.

"So what do our dear nobles have to say, counsellor?" Lurion asked, sarcastically.

"They seek audience of my lord, to complain of certain conditions in the city," he informed with some scorn.

"Do they? Well, times have changed have they not? I am not like Favro who pleased their fancies. They will soon see that I plan not to comfort their lives," Lurion said with disgust.

Two knocks sounded at the door and before Lurion could give his permission to enter, the doors opened and Rondree strode in dressed in his dark military uniform.

"Ah, Rondree, my faithful servant, how goes it? Do join us for lunch."

Rondree did not have a pleasant look on his face. For one reason, he did not like the king's counsellors and second he came with bad news. He bowed slightly and unwillingly at the king's guests and then respectfully to Lurion.

"Thank you, my Lord. But forgive me for interrupting your repast, but I have some unpleasant news."

Lurion's smile faded as he looked at Rondree's solemn stare.

"What is it?" he asked sternly.

"The Terandian army is on the march and coming towards us."

Anger quickly spread across the king's face. His counsellors also became very concerned over the news.

"The dung of Darnoof. Cursed be they," he said rising from his chair and pounding the table, rattling the plates and cups.

"Are they mad? Why do they come now?" The king left his chair and paced the floor not far from the table.

"We must recall our northern efforts, my king,"

said Rondree calmly but firmly.

"What! No! I want Dunen," he said furiously.

"Dunen can wait. Elena's army is sizeable to lay us an unwanted blow," Rondree returned.

"I would disagree, my Lord. They are no more than half of us and surely we can defeat them," said one of the counsellors confidently.

"Let them come indeed and we will be finished with them," said another proudly.

The king looked back and forth at them, uncertain of their opinions.

Rondree moved closer to the king, and being much taller, he loomed over him with a grave face.

"We cannot take any risk." Rondree whispered with a low and ominous voice.

"But, Dunen!" Lurion shot back in a strained whisper.

"We will have time for him later. The master will not appreciate our boldness if we fail and render his army deficient, my lord," Rondree told him.

Although being king, Lurion feared Rondree and respected his counsel more than anyone in his entourage. His fear of his master Ernum was even greater. He slowly moved away from Rondree's towering presence and seated himself with as much honour as he could.

"Rondree speaks well. Recall the army and prepare to meet the Terandians," he said without looking at Rondree or his counsellors.

"My lord is wise, and it shall be done immediately," Rondree then bowed to the king and before leaving, he bowed to the counsellors giving them a stare of disgust.

The two counsellors avoided his gaze as he passed.

The king turned to see him go out the door and a moment after, anger filled him. Glaring at his counsellors he shouted, "Out of here. Leave me alone!"

Nervously the counsellors bowed, left their places at the table and exited the chamber. Alone at the table, Lurion boiled with rage. As if speaking to his unseen enemy, Lurion shouted, "Cursed fools!"

Chapter 10
SUPPER WITH FRIENDS

It was evening in Maarkaat but torches lit the village grounds. Dunen was crossing the village and saluted the villagers as they passed one another. The people in return bowed with great respect. Mutual love grew between them from the recent events and from their common concern over Ernum and the future of the region of Elnoren. He was well received and felt at home. Dunen was impressed to see the people calm although news came that a large force of Lurion's army was marching towards them and war was soon to come to their peaceful valley. Many of them would certainly die, he thought. He felt burdened for bringing so much danger on such kind people. He moved among the homes and stopped at one. He felt a bit embarrassed and hesitated to knock.

A loud voice from inside came forth, "Enter Dunen, do not stand outside like a stalled ox," bellowed Bilob.

Dunen smiled with shame and entered.

Inside, the house was well lit; he saw a large table set for dinner. Some walls were draped and some were bare exposing the wooden planks that made up the walls. In one corner was a stone fireplace. A small fire was burning and a kettle was being heated. Dunen smelled the broth and hunger quickly came to him. Bilob's mother was by the fire and turned to welcome him, bowing low and slowly.

"Welcome, my lord to our humble home."

"It is my pleasure and a great honour to have been invited."

Mandara smiled happily for his kind words.

Bilob was couched on pillows.

"Come my friend and comfort yourself," he called, beckoning with his hand.

Dunen joined him and sat by his side.

"I'm glad to see you, my friend." Bilob said as he slapped Dunen hard on the shoulder.

"I am glad to have this time with you and your mother," he replied.

"And what about me?" Marani said as she entered the room. She wore a dress in shades of green and brown. With her red hair braided back, she looked beautiful and full of life. Dunen was surprised.

"Oh! Forgive me Marani. Bilob did not tell me that you would join us."

"Join you. I live here!" she said, finding his comment strange.

"Live here?" Dunen repeated being confused.

Then Marani understood the confusion. "Bilob did not tell you that he is my brother?"

Dunen's eyes widened with surprise and then turned to look at Bilob who had a dumbfounded stare.

"Did I not tell you she is my sister?" he said sheepishly.

"No!" Dunen answered disappointingly.

Bilob smiled stupidly.

"Bilob! What manners is this?" his mother shouted at him. "Forgive my son, Dunen. His belly is all what fills his mind."

Marani looked displeased with her brother.

"Forgive me Marani," Bilob could only say as he felt embarrassed.

Both women gave him an angry glare and then went into the kitchen.

"You are in trouble, my friend." Dunen chided.

"Indeed," he agreed and then asked him, "You also look troubled my friend?"

"Would you not be if many friends would soon perish?" Dunen revealed in a low tone so that the women would not hear.

"You blame yourself, but you have done nothing wrong, it is the Lord's doing. He has brought us together. We are willing to help, even die if need be. We would sooner or later have to deal with this Ernum. Do not trouble yourself."

Dunen was encouraged to hear this and was told the same by Celkob, but he still felt upset over the matter. Convincing himself he could do nothing now to change the coming events, he resigned himself to enjoy the evening with Bilob and his family.

Marani came soon and gave them both a drink.

"Thank you, Marani," he said as he gazed at her face.

He watched her leave and noticed that Bilob was watching him with a smirk of displeasure. Dunen gave him a dry smile.

Marani and her mother busied themselves and prepared the table. They soon were all seated and blessed the Lord for His goodness. As they ate, they spoke of the coming army, of the preparations for battle and of the other village warriors who joined them. The subject of course did not please Marani or her mother, and yet they graciously let the two talk of the matter. Later during their fellowship, Mandara forcefully changed the subject.

"Tell me Dunen. What are your customs in

Teranda? For I have heard many strange things and I know very little of your city but for my few visits to the market?"

"What customs do you find strange?" Dunen asked curiously.

"Concerning the royal family and the nobles. I hear that the mother chooses the bride for her sons. Is it so?" Mandara asked.

Marani began to feel uncomfortable at the question, but was also very interested.

"Yes that is true, in most cases, but the son must also agree. It is not well looked upon if the lady chosen to be the bride were not at peace with the mother. How do your men find wives?" he asked in return.

Bilob quickly cut in. "The men do the choosing," Bilob jumped in, in a bombastic way that made all look at him with surprise. "The father or the elder gives us wisdom and the mothers give wisdom to the daughters," he replied boastfully.

"And the mothers tell the fathers what wise words to say," Mandara added immediately.

Bilob gave a displeasing look at his mother while the others laughed. He then joined them.

After they all calmed down, Marani spoke. "I have been to Teranda as a child but only to the market with my mother. I will go one day and look upon the great buildings of stone. We are told that great men of skill carved the images that speak of many great stories of old and of Anandun. Is this true?" she asked Dunen.

"Yes it is true," he replied. "And if the Lord wills, I will invite you all for a visit."

This made them all happy to hear.

"I would like to visit the hall of warriors and the makers of swords. Your swords are magnificent and the envy of all. Each sword is made for the bearer, I heard. With those in the hands of our people, we would fight the day long and not tire," Bilob said with excitement.

"I will bring you myself, Bilob. It will be my pleasure and nothing compared to what you have done for me. You saved my life and I will never forget it," Dunen said gripping his huge arm.

Bilob was touched by his words and reached out also to grip Dunen's shoulder with his huge hand.

"You would have done the same, my friend," Bilob returned humbly.

Both women watched happy of the deepening friendship with Dunen.

"No. I would not," Dunen said seriously.

"What?" said Bilob pulling back his arm with

astonishment?

"You are too heavy to put on a horse," he replied sarcastically.

They all burst into laughter and Bilob watched with scorn over Dunen's jeering.

After an evening of well-needed fellowship, Dunen bid them good night and left their home. He began to walk back to his house and was happy for the pleasant time. He was thankful to the Lord for his new friends. The night sky was clear and stars twinkled brightly. Only a few villagers were moving around at this time. It was peaceful and yet war loomed ever closer on this village. This made his heart sink. Taking a longer route, he took time to speak with the Lord.

"Lord. I feel burdened by many things. I pray for these people and friends. Be with them in battle. I feel responsible for bringing this evil on them. Protect them and give them your strength. Help us to overcome them. Give us wisdom. I should not have come here; I should be with my people. Give peace to my mother and wisdom to the captains of the army."

Ending his pleas and thoughts to God, Dunen felt a little better. He knew the Lord had heard his prayer and would certainly do something for these good people. He returned to his home comforted and went to sleep.

Chapter 11
THE CHANGING TIDE

The next morning, much was being prepared for the battle in Maarkaat. Celkob and the tribal chiefs were gathered to discuss the battle to come. Dunen was with them and gave then much information on how the city soldiers would fight and their strategies. Outside, in several areas of the village, warriors practised fighting, riding and archery. With every hour that passed, many more warriors from other tribes entered Maarkaat. The village was full of activity as all busied themselves for the battle ahead.

Two warriors from Maarkaat rode swiftly into the village from the main road amidst the multitude. Dismounting before Celkob's house, they quickly entered, leaving the horses behind.

Within Celkob's home, several elders from the valley tribes were reclining on pillows, discussing among one another their part in the battle. Others, including Dunen, were standing around and were busy with the same task. The small house was filled with chatter until the two warriors abruptly entered.

Everyone halted their conversations as those assembled noticed the anxious faces of the messengers.

"My father, we have important news," exclaimed one anxiously.

"Speak," commanded Celkob.

"The enemy has turned away. They return to the city."

All were startled at the news and for a moment not a word was spoken. Then suddenly all spoke at the same time. Many began to praise the Lord for turning away the enemy and yet others, like Dunen, were very surprised and concerned. Dunen turned to look at Celkob and found he was already looking at him with the same disturbed expression. Then Celkob rose and raised his hand for silence. Slowly all silenced, and many looked on the village chief with interest.

"This may not be the time to rejoice. We know not why they have turned away."

For a moment, all wondered of his warning, then agreed that something odd had occurred. Some felt a little embarrassed for reacting so prematurely.

"Then what does this mean?" asked one of the elders.

"Why would they come so near only to turn back?"

asked another, turning to Dunen. Speculation began to rise among them.

"Dunen, have you any knowledge about why they would have abandoned their course?" asked Celkob.

All fell silent again and waited for Dunen's words with great interest. Dunen's thoughts were racing to find an answer to the turn of events.

"I am not sure," he told them hesitantly.

Having been taught the art of war as a prince in the palace, he knew that only a greater obstacle could persuade the enemy to change its plans. He feared that maybe Lurion had discovered the whereabouts of his father's army, and was now gathering to destroy it. For the moment, Dunen was relieved that the villagers would not have to fight his war, but now he feared for his people's well being. Dunen now struggled with the thought of asking for their help, but was not willing to see his new friends pay for his family's error with their blood.

The elders continued their discussion and wondered at the change of events.

"We must continue to prepare ourselves and wait for news," one of the other elders said, and many agreed.

"They may yet return, and we must be ready," said another.

"That would be wise, and so it shall be done," Celkob added in agreement.

"Send some that will watch and warn us of their movements. And if we can find out their plans, all the better," another leader gave his advice.

"Derlob," Celkob commanded a villager near the door. "Have two swift riders follow and give us news."

Derlob departed immediately.

Dunen was encouraged to see the villager's continued interest in this uncertain struggle. He hoped he was wrong about the reason for the enemy's retreating army. Further news would help the situation.

#

Farther south, the Terandian army marched along the King's road leading to Teranda. Six horsemen, three side by side, proudly displayed the royal banners and emblems as they led the long troop. A small company of royal court soldiers followed them, and not too far behind came Queen Elena and her captains. The greater part of the army marched on foot behind their leaders, followed closely after by the cavalry and the carts carrying the army's supplies and materials. Menfre and the three captains rode beside their queen.

"Beyond the next hill we come to the fields of Moridir," Menfre informed Elena in a solemn voice.

She did not look at him, but stared ahead. Her thoughts were much in prayer that all would go well. She hoped that if Dunen lived, he would understand why Lurion had turned back from pursuing him. She was also very troubled by the battle ahead but with great effort, she hid her feelings from her captains. Her hope rested completely on the Lord's mercy.

Just as Menfre had said, the forest soon opened, and the army arrived at the fields of Moridir. This large open space had witnessed many battles, and the blood of many ran deep in the soil. The field was flat and accommodated two armies on opposite sides. Quickly and calmly the Terandian army spread itself out and prepared to camp. The first tents to go up belonged to the Queen and her captains.

Much planning and decision-making was still needed for the upcoming battle. Lurion's army would not arrive until the early hours of the next day. This would give their foot soldiers a slight advantage of a nights rest, but no more.

After the soldiers had set up camp, the army of men settled down as the soldiers slowly lay down to sleep after a time of fellowship and preparing their weapons. The only ones who remained awake in the late evening were the camp sentinels, the captains, and Queen Elena.

Chapter 12
THE BATTLE OF MORIDIR

In the early morning hours, Queen Elena's army awoke and prepared for battle. As expected, news came of the approach of Lurion's army. The camp busied itself and then placed itself in order. Just as the sun rose, a small rumble grew across the field as Lurion's army entered Moridir from the north. The Terandians watched as the enemy spread across the opposite field and made camp. Lurion's army, more than twice the size of theirs, dismayed the onlookers. By midday, Lurion's army could be seen preparing for battle.

In the captain's tent, much was now being discussed as the time approached. The orders were given out to assemble the army for battle. As the Terandian army placed itself on the field, Menfre, Shadly and Manru put on their battle armour. Their casks were laid aside as they pored over the battlefield map on the centre table for one last time.

"The archers must have a clear shot when called upon, this must be understood by all," Manru said seriously.

"It will be as you say," answered Menfre.

"They must be prepared to come quickly to our aid

if any weakness occurs in the ranks," said Shadly, "or else a breach would bring a deadly blow."

The two other men nodded.

"Order your men not to push beyond the line. We need not take any chances. We must gain time if we hold today," Menfre said.

"I am not concerned for today, Menfre," Shadly said confidently. "I fear tomorrow's battle."

"Well, then, let us rise and be strong and fight for our God," Menfre said encouragingly.

The others straightened and held their heads high at the call. Placing their helmets on, they strode out of the tent, following Menfre. Several officers came and spoke with Menfre on last minute details as he emerged. The discussions over, he got on his horse. Danar, coming from other affairs in the camp, led his horse beside his peers. It was midday and the sun shone strongly. The armour glittered in the sun as the army was called to rise and form their ranks. A great number of foot soldiers readied and made three rows the length of the camp. Their shields were set before them, their swords not yet unsheathed. On command they moved forward a few paces and stopped.

The archers were then summoned and took position behind the foot soldiers, leaving a gap between them, their bows strapped around their shoulders and the quivers full of arrows. Once again a signal was given and both lines moved forward fifty paces. The cavalry now rode into place behind the archers and stood still. The horses seemed anxious as they stamped the ground, their nostrils flaring fiercely and ready to ride into battle. Thick leather pads protected their heads and necks, and brightly colored patterned quilts covered their bodies.

Menfre and his captains came riding upright and strong in their saddles as they inspected the Terandian army.

The soldiers stood before their captains with great pride, determination, and honour as they passed.

Across the field, the enemy was setting themselves in array and matched the length of the Terandian army, but with deeper numbers.

As the captains completed their inspection, they halted at the forefront of the army. From the camp, three horsemen bearing the Terandian banners and emblems circled the lines and joined the captains. Lady Elena, riding on a white stallion, followed them not far behind. Gallantly she sat on her horse with uprightness. She was dressed in a bright dress of gold with blue trimmings, and a red belt holding a short sword. A handkerchief with a band across her forehead barely covered her long and flowing hair. All eyes were on her as she halted before the army. She gave her captains an encouraging nod and then faced the army.

The army gave a great shout and cheered for Elena. A smile of great appreciation came over Elena and the captains. After a long cheer, the army quieted down.

"This is your day for Teranda," she said speaking as loudly as she could. "A day we must manifest our strength as well as our love," she said and paused for a moment before going on.

"Our love for our God and for our people. We have come to challenge and to overcome this evil that has entered our land and wickedly taken our homes. The Lord will be our strength, and we will fight valiantly. From my heart I tell you, I have no greater joy than to be amidst so good and noble men."

The whole army erupted with a great cheer and then quieted to hear more from their beloved queen.

"Be strong and of good courage, for it is the Lord's battle," Elena finished and rode off back behind the ranks and saluted her men and they saluted her in return.

Menfre gave the signal and a horseman raised his trumpet and gave the sound to move forward. The foot soldiers marched forth, all three lines in unison. After a pause, the archers followed and then the cavalry.

Across the field, Lurion's army responded by moving forward as well, their darkened armor creating a sullen and menacing wall. Rondree had sent five lines of foot soldiers and two lines of archers ahead. Behind them awaited two more lines of foot soldiers, followed by a line of cavalry.

Rondree's face looked grim and confident. Looking on the Terandian army, Rondree sneered with confidence over this unequal match.

Within three hundred paces, the flagmen and captains halted as the foot soldiers came from behind, passed them by and went on before them. The archers as well went by. They then continued their march in between the line of foot soldiers and the horsemen.

On their opponent's side, Rondree and his captains could be seen riding behind their soldiers as well.

As the two armies approached, the foot soldiers drew their swords. Soon after, the archers took in hand their bows; each fitted an arrow to the string and let loose. Immediately, several volleys of arrows streamed from either side across the battlefield. Shields were raised for cover, and yet some of the arrows found a place to inflict injury and death. The cries of men began.

All along both sides, both armies continued to press forward. At thirty paces, as if a signal was given, the Terandian soldiers raised a shout and attacked. The foot soldiers of both armies came crashing against each other with a great clash of swords against swords and shields. The captains spread themselves out to oversee the battle. The Terandians fought valiantly as they held their ranks and returned many losses to the enemy. Rondree, yelling orders to his men, was angered by the strength of his opponents. Menfre, likewise, went around shouting orders and strengthening his men.

As time swiftly passed in the great struggle, Menfre ordered Danar to send his archers and refresh the foot soldiers. Injured soldiers were drawn from the battle and taken to camp to be cared for. The battle went well for the Terandians, trained and hearty men. As the light of day began to wane, Teranda's men began to weaken, but it was not long before the day drew to a close and the sun began its descent above the trees, and dusk slowly came across the battlefield. Menfre ordered the trumpeter to sound the retreat. Both armies disengaged, cautiously marching backwards from the battle line, leaving behind a line of many felled men. The armies slowly returned to camp as servants came to recover the dead and take care of the injured. Menfre and the captains rode around, overseeing the placement and care of the men. At the same time, reports began to come in concerning the day's battle.

After all quieted down within the camp and night fell, there was still much activity in the command tent. The captains were united to review the day's battle. Reports continued to flow in from the field officers concerning the men, the weapons, and how the enemy had fought. Torches lit the room as Shadly paced about, his fingers nervously gripping the pommel of his sword as his shadow danced against the walls. Menfre was seated calmly at the table with Danar. Manru was absent, as he tended to certain affairs in the camp.

"We fared well today. Our casualties are half what

we have inflicted upon them," Danar said looking over a report given to him.

"Hmm, it was as we expected, but tomorrow will be different," Menfre said with concern.

Shadly stopped his pacing to answer him, "Tomorrow will be a long day. We have none to replace those who fought today. They have a second line of ready men. We will weaken by midday, is my guess," he replied solemnly.

Menfre and Danar did not like the assessment but agreed sombrely.

"We must consider withdrawing from the battle," Shadly brought out hesitantly.

"And be cut down as we escape? Never!" said Danar fervently. "I would rather die facing my enemy."

"Even if we live to see the day after, we will be destroyed with little effort the next day! Do you disagree?" Shadly quickly returned, facing Danar. "We have done what we could. If Lurion was seeking Dunen, we have altered his plans. We need not stay but one day longer."

"Shadly speaks well," Menfre stated. "We need not come to our end here and now. Tomorrow we will fight and hope for the night. If we still stand, we withdraw."

"It will be the first time that Teranda retreats from a fight," Danar said solemnly and all were disgusted by the thought.

"We have no choice. We must preserve something for another day," Shadly concluded.

"So be it. I will inform Lady Elena. Danar, you will arrange for the Queen's escape if it goes ill for us," Menfre commanded unhappily.

"It will be done."

All three left the tent to retire for the evening. Their faces were grave and saddened over the plans they had unwillingly set forth.

The morning brought a cloudy and gloomy day, as if the sky was saddened by the events below its canopy. The camp was filled with the smell of breakfast as the soldiers ate in small groups all over the field. Slowly the camp livened as they began their preparations for the day's battle. Horses were equipped and saddled. Archers again filled their quivers full of arrows and soldiers put on their armor and attached swords to their belts. Field officers shouted commands across the camp as men hurried in obedience.

Menfre and Danar exited the command tent and

moved off towards the horses. Officers joined them for a short moment to receive last-minute details from the captains. Shadly and Manru rode towards them, after completing certain duties.

"As best we can, we must delay going into combat. We must gain time. One hour could make all the difference," Menfre told his captains.

They nodded in agreement but disliked the weak ploy.

"The officers have been told," confirmed Shadly.

Across the battlefield, Lurion's army had set themselves in array and waited for their opponents. The Terandian army, in return, gradually took their positions. An hour or so passed as finally they came into order as on the previous day. As Menfre and the captains slowly inspected the ranks, an officer informed them that the enemy had begun to move forward.

"Impatient with our game. Then so be it. Let us go forth," said Menfre, attempting to speak boldly, but disturbed that the day's battle had begun. "The Lord be with us. Sound to march!"

The trumpet sounded and the foot soldiers began their advance as the rest followed.

Once again, archers on both sides sent their deadly

darts across the field. After several volleys, Menfre drew out his sword, and looking at Manru, raised it above him.

Manru withdrew his sword on Menfre's order and commanded his horsemen to prepare to attack. At once the horsemen unsheathed their swords and waited on their captain. Assured that all his horsemen were ready, he looked towards the enemy defiantly and pointed his sword at them. A trumpet sounded and the horses sprang forward. With a great shout, Manru led the attack.

On hearing the trumpet, the foot soldiers broke ranks, leaving space for the horsemen to pass through. Rondree, seeing the coming cavalry, ordered his horsemen to confront them. Drawing his sword, he shouted and went forth, leading them across their own soldiers.

Both cavalry raced towards each other with the thundering of horse's hooves beating the ground. Crossing the narrow field swiftly, they soon crashed into one another. Men were cut down as they streaked across each other, failing to block the fatal blows. The cries of horses filled the air as they came against each other, some being stabbed by the swords and some lamed by crashing into other horses.

Rondree quickly dispatched his first opponent and engaged another. Menfre and his captains fought with fervour, and with great skill, quickly defeating their opponents. Some even drew back as they encountered them, fearing the master swordsmen.

The foot soldiers, not far behind, soon entered the fray with a roar of clashing metal and shields. The shouts and cries of men loudly proclaimed the terrible struggle. A great commotion of men and horses moved across the field. Little by little, the horsemen retreated to allow the foot soldiers to fight.

Menfre, Shadly, Danar and Manru soon gathered themselves together. Their armor were smeared with blood and great streams of sweat ran down their faces. Wiping their bloodied blades on their legs, they then returned them to their scabbards.

"Well done, my friends," Menfre proclaimed between breaths. "The horses should now be returned to camp, and a line should be readied to replace our soldiers."

"Yea, my captain. I will see to it," Manru replied and immediately departed, shouting orders to the waiting cavalry.

"Danar, the archers must do likewise, but keep a remnant for safety," Menfre commanded.

"We shall be prepared," Danar answered and galloped off.

Menfre relaxed himself on his horse a little and viewed the battle.

"I am beginning to doubt we can hold the day," Menfre told Shadly.

"We must and we shall, by God's grace," Shadly replied ardently.

Menfre gave him a smile for his zeal and then returned to see how the battle faired.

"When necessary, begin to replace those who fight at your discretion. Danar's men will soon be ready," Menfre commanded Shadly.

"Yea, at once, my captain." Shadly turned his horse around and left his captain.

Menfre was now alone, and continued to examine the fight. This was a great and costly struggle, he thought, and doubt came to his mind. Did he do the right thing? Was it the Lord's will? Was it the right time? Had he brought his master's army to ruin?

"Lord! Have mercy upon us. Manifest your hand, Lord of Hosts," he asked, looking into the sky at the unseen God.

Elena, not far from her tent, looked on the battle with anxiety. Soon injured men were carried into the camp to be cared for. Turning away her attention from the battle, compassionately she joined the servants to help care for the men.

Not long after, Manru and Danar returned to the battle line with ready soldiers. Menfre urged them to spread out across the field and place themselves under the leadership of Shadly. Immediately they dispersed.

As the battle drew on, tired and injured soldiers came forth from the battle and were replaced by others. Some dropped to the ground with exhaustion not far from where they fought; others lay down to rest. Menfre dismounted his horse and moved among them, speaking to some and encouraging others. Many more were relieved from their struggles and found a place to rest across the field. Servants appeared from the camp bringing water and bandages.

Menfre came to one soldier and asked him how it went.

"We are holding our own, but forgive me, captain,

if I ask, for how long?" he inquired, out of breath, aching with bruises and cuts. "They have another two more columns of men that have not as yet seen battle. We will be cut to pieces when they come!"

Menfre listened, and anguish tore at his heart. "We must make it through this day," he said, looking up at the sky, "We have but a few more hours."

"Yea, but what of tomorrow?" the soldier questioned, looking at the captain with worry and pain.

"We retreat tonight, if we can," Menfre told him.

The soldier was surprised at first but then accepted the news. "Then surely we must be strong. I will give my all against these filthy dogs!" the soldier spat fervently.

"Good, my brother. Be of good cheer, they will not have us yet," Menfre said squeezing his shoulder.

A comforted smile came over the soldier's dirty and perspiring face.

Menfre continued his visit among the men, and all of sudden a great cry of men rose at one end of the battle. Menfre turned to see a breach occur in the battle line. Lurion's soldiers pierced through the ranks. Not far away, Shadly quickly charged at the enemy with violent strokes of his sword that slew several before they could know what fell on them. Other soldiers joined him, and those who rested rose to resist the flood until other soldiers could force back the enemy and strengthen the line. When the foray ended, Shadly was found on the ground, one amongst the slain of both camps. Menfre and others ran to him and knelt by his side.

"Shadly! My brother," Menfre turned him around to lay him on his back. Two stabs, one near the heart, could now be seen, where a sword had found its way through the armor. Blood poured from Shadly's mouth as he tried to speak.

"Is all well?" he asked, in pain.

"Yes," Menfre replied, trembling with anguish.

Shadly answered with a quick and bloodied smile.

"Good. Be strong." His voice wavered with pain. "The men have done well. They fight valiantly. But for me, no more battles I fight - peace awaits me," he said. With a feeble but peaceful expression, he gave his last breath and died.

Menfre stood still as he looked on his friend. A great grief and emptiness filled his heart for the loss of his friend.

"Know that my love goes with you, dear friend," he said as tears rolled down his cheeks. "Here lies a mighty man of valour. A great heart for his people and for his God. Mighty in good deeds and a faithful soldier. He will be remembered," Menfre bowed his head in grief and then got up.

Servants who stood nearby watched the sad scene and were ready to take away the body. Menfre turned and walked away. Wiping away his tears, he returned to the battle with renewed anger. Finding Danar running around, he grabbed him roughly.

"How goes it?" Menfre demanded.

Danar perceived Menfre's angered face and knew something terrible had occurred, "What has happened?" he asked.

"Shadly is dead."

Danar's eyes widened with shock and then with grief. Menfre grabbed his shoulder forcefully. "Let us continue the work. What are the conditions?"

Danar tried to respond, his thoughts disturbed by the news. "We keep them at bay, but the men tire quickly," he replied.

"Menfre!" Elena cried as she approached them, moving fearlessly among the soldiers who rested on the field. "What tidings have you?"

"The men are weakening."

Instead of being troubled by the news, she frowned and became roused with determination. "I must encourage them. Fetch me a horse," she commanded Menfre.

"It is not safe my lady."

"These are my men! Fetch my horse," she demanded fiercely.

Hesitating for a moment, Menfre did not like to see the Queen of Teranda riding dangerously in the midst of a battle, but he knew he could not change her mind. Menfre ordered two horses to be brought. Soon Elena and Menfre were mounted. Elena, with a zealous spirit, kicked her horse into a gallop and rode along the line of battle.

"Fight, my good men! Fight for your God and your people!" she shouted to the men.

The soldiers, hearing her call, gathered their strength and, with a shout, struck forward. The enemy moved back by the renewed vigor, but yielded momentarily.

Rondree watched the queen's efforts with disdain and scorn.

"Shout with all of your heart, dear lady, if it will honour your end," he said to himself as he watched her frantically riding and shouting to her men.

The soldiers, roused by her cry, strengthened themselves and fought harder. Up and down the line Elena rode while encouraging her soldiers.

Menfre, excited by her zeal, took courage and joined her.

Rondree signalled for the second line to move forward.
"It is time to end this," he said confidently.
Two long lines of fresh soldiers boldly moved forward and approached the battle line.

As Elena stopped and saw the strong new lines of soldiers approaching, he heart sank as she understood this would mean the end.
Then a flash of light caught her attention from the corner of her eye. Curiously, she looked at the flickering light coming from the north-western tip of the enemy camp.
On a hill bordering the forest, she saw a lone horseman. The horseman could be seen waving a sword above his head and wearing a gleaming coat of armor. Instantly, Elena's heart leaped as she recognised Dunen.
"Dunen! My son," she could only whisper his to herself, overwhelmed by his appearance and then she began to shout with immense joy.
"Dunen! Dunen!" she cried out louder and louder.
Her shouts caught the attention from the soldiers

around her.

Menfre, hearing her cry, looked in the same direction and saw Dunen.

Immediately, he shouted, "King Dunen! King Dunen!" with great joy and relief. "Praise God, Lord of hosts!"

Rondree turned his horse around and saw Dunen as well. At that same moment, a dark shadow of moving shapes rose behind Dunen. The shapes became visible as they emerged from the forest shadow and revealed a great host of horsemen. They aligned themselves to the right and to the left of Dunen, growing ever more in number.

Rondree immediately ordered the reserve foot soldiers to turn around and face the new forces.

"Let the son of Favro come to me," Rondree commanded his captains.

Hearing of Dunen's arrival, the Terandian army shouted with great excitement, troubling the enemy lines and augmenting their zeal in combat.

Dunen, with a great charge, led the attack, followed by the great cries of the tribesmen and the ringing of swords being drawn from their scabbards. Riding beside Dunen was Bilob, his face ablaze with fierceness. In a moment, the menacing wall of tribesmen rushed towards the battlefield.

Their great horses pounded the ground and filled the air with a mighty thunder. Before reaching the enemy lines, some tribesmen jumped off their horses to fight on foot.

Dunen, remaining on his horse, was given passage across the enemy line to confront his adversary. Rondree calmly seated on his horse, waited for him, his gleaming sword in his hand and lying across his stirrup. Dunen's anger rose as he approached Rondree and quickly engaged him with a hard blow. With ease, Rondree deterred the onslaught.

"You have decided to stop your running, Dunen," he said with a sneer.

Rondree's words augmented Dunen's hatred, and moved him to strike again with enraged force. Rondree blocked the strikes and returned with several swings that forced Dunen to retreat.

"By coming to me, you have saved me the trouble of finding you," Rondree said maliciously. "For this, I thank you."

"You will regret my visit, son of Cain," Dunen returned.

Moving their horses into position, they continued to strike at each other. Rondree, with a strong thrust, was able to push Dunen off his horse and send him to the ground.

Elena watched her son's combat with great fear and screamed as she saw Dunen being thrown off his horse.

"Dunen!" she cried out. His horse obstructed her view as she anxiously looked for a sign of his condition.

Dunen rolled away from his troubled horse before he got trampled, and raised himself from the ground. Rondree laughed and dismounted his horse. Both men faced each other as the battle raged around them. Dunen watched Rondree carefully and moved around cautiously; knowing Rondree was older and a more experienced swordsman of the two.

"You should have stayed hidden with your friends!" Rondree said menacingly as he drew near to Dunen.

"You will die from my hand and no other!" Dunen forewarned him, and then struck.

Both men engaged each other and returned blows. Dunen on several occasions sent his opponent back, and swiftly defended himself from the deadly counter-strikes.

Rondree paused and laughed. "A brave effort, but foolhardy."

"Who truly is the fool? I live free but you live a slave to Ernum. You have but death that awaits you and darkness for eternity."

Rondree, enraged by his words, struck forward with a violent swing of his sword that sent Dunen to the ground.

Quickly Dunen rolled away as Rondree stabbed the ground where he once lay. Having a moment to think, Dunen remembered his duel with Bilob, and the strategy he used to win. Dunen raised himself and confronted Rondree's advance and wild swings. Rondree withstood his attack and Dunen returned with swift, strong blows. Rondree, angered by the onslaught, struck back in return. After several blows, Dunen struck upward, giving Rondree an opportunity. Rondree, seeing the opening, stabbed at Dunen's chest. Dunen quickly turned his body parallel to the oncoming sword, which bounced off his breastplate. At that same moment, Dunen shifted his sword in his hand and drove the blade in his exposed side joints of armour.

Rondree cried aloud with pain and dropped his sword as he moved away. His face was mixed with surprise and agony. Dunen then thrust his sword through his chest.

Rondree stared at Dunen a moment with a bitter hate and then fell dead to the ground.

Dunen stood sweating and tired as he gazed at his dead opponent, relieved that it was over. A great shout brought his attention to the battle.

The tribesmen, with their mighty strength and spirit, overwhelmed their enemies and broke through the lines. Lurion's army, confused and overcome by the tribesmen, gave way and scattered.

With Rondree dead and his captains dismayed by the overwhelming forces, the enemy forces lost their will to fight and fled before their adversaries. The tribesmen and the Terandians pursued them, striking many down as they retreated. Great shouting rose as victory was theirs.

Elena, finding a way open, went to Dunen. With great joy, Dunen ran to meet his mother, helped her off her horse and then embraced her.

Elena, cried with joy, kissed him on the cheek and caressed his face.

"My son!" she said happily.

"Mother," he could only say as he cried with joy.

"I feared for your life my love," she said trembling with relief.

"And I for yours," he told her and said, "I did not

want to leave. I did not want to leave Father-" he stopped, unable to explain his reasons.

"You did well, my son. You stayed alive," Elena comforted him.

He looked on her smiling face and felt a heavy weight of guilt leave him. He hugged her and buried his face in her neck.

"All is well now, my son. You have done well," she said as she stroked his hair.

Menfre soon arrived at the scene.

"My lord! My king," Menfre said as he jumped off his horse. Immediately he got to one knee before him, bowed and looked up at his master. "The Lord be blessed. You live and have come to our rescue."

Dunen grabbed Menfre's shoulder, and then both embraced each other heartily.

"What blessed joy to see you, Menfre," Dunen told him.

"You have come just in time, and with such an army of warriors. How were you able to muster so great a company?" Menfre wondered, looking at the tribesmen as they fought the enemy.

"The Lord's doing and a long story my friend."

"I doubt it not and I am eager to hear it."

Bilob soon trotted up to the small company and

halted before them, his sword, tainted with blood, still in his large hand.

"Is all well, Dunen?" Bilob asked as he breathed heavily from his fighting.

"I should ask you," Dunen answered instead.

"I-" he began to answer, but stopped and was surprised the moment he saw Elena, "This is your mother," he asked.

"Yes," Dunen replied.

Bilob bowed in his saddle. "I am Bilob, from the village of Maarkaat. It is a great honour to meet the mother of my friend, and the well-known Queen of Teranda."

"Your most kind," Queen Elena said graciously. "And I welcome you, Bilob, and your good people on behalf of Teranda, as dear friends."

Bilob bowed from his saddle with deep esteem.

"And I thank you deeply for protecting my son and coming to our aid," she said as she happily looked on her son.

"We are your servants and old friends," he said proudly.

"You have given us a victory, my brother." Dunen told him.

"A great victory!" Bilob shouted happily.

"I agree," he said and laughed at his friend's zeal.

"I must return to the fight." Bilob said and sprinted off after a short bow.

Dunen and Elena were left alone and she looked at her son.

"You have your father's sword," Elena said as she noticed Dunen's sword.

Dunen lifted the sword. "Yes. I will tell you later how it came into my hands," he said solemnly.

Elena nodded, knowing very well that her son carried within his heart a terrible story, one in which he needed to share.

"In due time my son," she comforted him compassionately.

Chapter 13
THE RIGHTFUL KING

Early next morning, Dunen, his mother, Bilob, Celkob and the captains were gathered in the command tent. All were standing around the table as they listened to Manru, who had recently come from Teranda.

"Lurion has declared he will not yield the throne to Dunen," Manru stated flatly.

All were not happy with the news.

"He is mad!" said Danar.

"His army is destroyed and he has at most a thousand soldiers guarding the city. He cannot believe to survive a siege for long," Elena wondered in frustration.

"I guess my lady that he waits for Ernum to send help," Menfre suggested.

They all agreed and worried at the thought.

"True, we must take the city immediately and rebuild our forces as soon as we can. Ernum has forces greater than our own. Without the city, we are sure to invite him," Dunen added.

"I will gather those who are able to fight and prepare to ride at your command, my lord," Danar said as he rose to leave.

Celkob and Bilob gave each other a quizzical look.

"How will you overcome the great walls of your city with the forces at hand?" Celkob questioned, "Even if we try to build ladders, we will fail."

The Terandians smiled with embarrassment.

"Forgive us, Celkob. We speak what we know, and you are not aware of a secret among us. My great-grandfather Anandun, who built the city walls, made sure of their strength for defence, but also left ways in which, upon need, we could enter the city. None but my family and loyal advisers know of these secrets."

Bilob was bewildered. "Dunen, if you speak of that little passage through the wall, you are beside yourself! Only a few men may go in at one time, you will be slaughtered as you come out."

Dunen smiled. "There is another way, Bilob. But I must keep it secret till it is time. If the enemy was warned, all hope would be lost to regain the city."

"Even if our entrance be easy, the fight will not. Let us be careful," Menfre warned them.

"Let us ride for Teranda," Dunen ordered.

They all nodded with determination and exited the tent. Menfre, Danar and Manru began shouting orders to the officers. Immediately the camp moved with excitement. Horses were readied and soldiers prepared their armor. The tribesmen as well, ordered by Celkob and Bilob, prepared to ride.

In a short time, the horsemen bearing the banners and emblems led the way, followed by Dunen, his mother and the captains. The tribal leaders and a great number of horsemen followed behind. Leaving the camp and passing by the deserted enemy camp, they took the road that led westward toward Teranda. They quickly urged their horses from a trot to a gallop and sped along. Gravely and resolutely they travelled the road, side by side, a great company of men with armor glittering in the sun. The pounding of the horse's hooves shook the ground as they rode by.

At midday, the company halted for a short time to give the horses some rest. Some took the time to eat, while others brought the horses to a nearby stream for water. Many entered the water to bathe and wash away the dirt of the road.

Dunen sat on a rock near the river and was thinking on the coming attack on his city and his past. His mother approached him, laid her hand on his dark brown hair and caressed it.

"What is upon your heart, my son?" She asked.

"Father and Tharan," he answered.

"I cannot forget them, either," she said sadly.

"I also wonder about the future. There is so much evil abounding, how will we resist?" He wondered.

"I do not know, but we must find a way," she told him with a smile. "You must not worry for the future. Do what is in your power today. The Lord will lead you for tomorrow and be with you when it comes."

Dunen smiled with encouragement, happy to be with his mother again and to receive her tenderness and wisdom.

Not long after, a trumpet called them to mount, and in a short time they continued their journey.

As they drew closer to Teranda, the surprised farmers and peasants waved and cheered as they recognized the army of Teranda and the royal family.

Slowly the road rose as it led further into the mountains. Farmers quickly moved their wagons aside at the approaching army. After a long road upward, following the curves of the southern mountain range, they came to the city. The sound of their arrival echoed against the walls and resounded along the mountainsides. On Menfre's command, the army remained out of reach of the enemy's arrows, and a line was formed facing the wall.

On the wall, Lurion's soldiers looked on, the archers visible between the openings. The wooden gates loomed high within an arch of grey stone. Lurion's banners and flags fluttered atop the walls, to the disgust of the Terandians. The noise died down as the army came to a halt before the walls. Dunen asked for a shield and soon it was given to him.

"Be careful, my son," Elena said to him with concern.

"I shall, mother," Dunen replied and then kicked his horse forward.

Leaving the army behind, he moved slowly toward the wall and halted.

"Hear, you who guard the city of Teranda. I am Dunen, son of King Favro. Your master Lurion has by wicked hands usurped the throne of my father and has killed many righteous people," he said loudly to the enemy on the walls as he looked carefully to the right of the main gates, refreshing his memory for the location of the secret keyhole.

"I have defeated your army and now come to claim the throne which rightly belongs to me!" he continued. "I command you to surrender your arms and open the gate! If you obey, I promise to spare your lives."

Not a second passed before arrows whistled by and struck the ground nearby. Dunen raised his shield and turned away two arrows destined for him.

One arrow found its way into the horse's neck. The horse leaped into the air with a cry and sent Dunen to the ground. Elena refrained from crying out, but whispered Dunen's name with fright. The captains and others who watched the scene were angered and eager to strike back. Dunen's horse bolted off wildly, leaving him alone on the field. Quickly he sought refuge behind his shield as other arrows continued to rain down. His friends nervously looked on but were relieved to see him unharmed.

"He would not let me do this!" Menfre told Elena while hiding his fear.

Elena knew that Dunen wanted to do this himself, even at his peril.

Gathering his wits, Dunen then rushed to the wall. The archers, with difficulty, continued to shoot as he reached the stone wall. Dunen, placing his shield above him, thwarted the arrows as he felt along the wall for the hole. Remembering how many times his father taught him how to find the secret hole, brought longing memories of him.

Finding the familiar grooves, he drew his sword. With some difficulty, he slid the sword into the stone wall all the way to the hilt and then withdrew it. With his back to the wall, he signalled his army.

"Yea, stand ready!" Menfre shouted to the soldiers and drew his sword. The riders followed suit and unsheathed their swords as archers readied their bows.

A great bang came forth from the walls near the gates. The soldiers on the wall stopped shooting at Dunen as they heard the strange sounds. Several more great bangs occurred and shook the walls. Suddenly the frame that held the great wooden doors broke away from the wall, and fell forward to the ground with a great earth-shaking crash. A huge cloud of dust rose from the ground and engulfed Dunen.

"Teranda!" Shouted Menfre and then kicked his horse forward. With a momentous cry the whole army streamed toward the open entrance. The enemy sent forth their arrows again but with little effect. In moments the army entered the city and engaged Lurion's soldiers. The Terandian archers quickly killed the soldiers on the wall.

Danar and Bilob, leaving the troop, went to Dunen,

who remained beside the wall.

"Come, my lord, ride with me," Danar said, stretching out his hand.

Quickly Dunen mounted behind him.

"By Nurob's sword, this will be a tale to be told to our children and grandchildren forever!" Bilob declared with awe and excitement.

"Ride on Danar. To the palace," Dunen instructed him.

Danar turned his horse around and galloped into the city. Fighting continued, but Lurion's soldiers were now on the run. The people of the city remained in their homes, afraid of the great tumult, yet some were bold enough to wave and shout for joy from their windows and doors. Dunen quickly ordered his soldiers to follow him to the palace. With great speed they rode along the narrow cobblestone road, the horse's hooves clattering and echoing within the walled lanes.

As Dunen passed the familiar road to Aristinne's home, he wondered what had happened to her and her family during Teranda's fall. He hoped they were well.

Approaching the centre of the city, the great company exited the main road and entered the great palace square. The riders quickly flooded into the inner court and spread out, ready to encounter hostile forces, but no challenge came.

Dunen dismounted with Danar and Bilob. Celkob also joined him before the steps.

"Let us enter first, my lord, for wicked traps may await us yet," Danar warned.

"Go, but be careful. I will follow."

Soon Danar ordered soldiers to enter the palace. With caution they opened the unlocked doors and rushed in. Moments later, a soldier signalled that all was well within the palace entrance. Dunen and the others joined them.

Inside, Bilob and Celkob looked around with great wonder on the stone arches, carvings, and picturesque marble floor. As the soldiers moved within the palace searching for hidden enemies, they all drew nigh to the throne room. The doors to the hall were made of burgundy wood with latches of gold, and their height was about twelve feet. When opened, not a sound could be heard from them as they turned on the well balanced hinges.

At the far end of the hall, to everyone's surprise, Lurion was seated on the throne. Dunen's soldiers entered and carefully searched the hall, while several of them came swiftly before Lurion, surrounding him with their swords pointing toward him menacingly. Lurion, oddly, paid no attention to them as he stared continually at Dunen as he approached. His face was gaunt and his manner slow, as if he had just awakened.

Dunen, followed by the others, came to the steps of the throne. A great anger welled up inside Dunen against Lurion, but he tried to control it.

"Lurion, you are defeated. I reclaim my father's throne."

"You may have it. I give no resistance," Lurion said, sounding weak and disinterested.

"You are a traitor to the people of Teranda, and a murderer! You will be tried and put to death," Dunen could only say.

Lurion smiled to himself as if remembering a joke.

Dunen realized Lurion was not acting normally, and a thought came to his mind.

"Why are you still here? Your army was defeated!"

"Where would I go?" Lurion asked slowly. "I have failed. If I run, Ernum would find me. Yes, you cannot escape him," he informed him. "I am better off dead." His face jerked briefly with some unknown pain and then returned to normal.

"You will be judged and beheaded before he can touch you. This I assure you," Dunen told him emphatically.

"I do not think I will have the time for that. I have taken some poison and will soon die," Lurion said with a wry smile.

All who heard were struck with amazement.

"Take him away from my face," Dunen said, troubled by what he heard.

The soldiers came and took him.

"Wait! Before I go, accord me one wish," Lurion begged Dunen, rousing himself briefly.

Dunen was astonished at his audacity, but was curious to know what he wanted. "What is it?"

"Do not bury me. I wish to be burned. Ernum will seek my body even in the grave," Lurion said with horror. "Please, burn me."

"Do as he wishes, but outside the city," Dunen commanded.

While the soldiers took Lurion away, Dunen watched him go and was greatly troubled. He could not believe the wickedness of Ernum, nor the fear he evoked on his servants. This made Dunen fear all the more of Ernum and his plans.

Menfre entered the hall with a troop of soldiers.

"The city is ours, my lord. Lurion's soldiers have been defeated."

"Very good," Dunen replied, still affected by Lurion's words.

"The throne, my lord, is now yours," Danar said happily.

Dunen turned to look at the golden chair with its burgundy padded armrests and intricate carved designs. Inscriptions of ancient words were also carved within the gold. Dunen contemplated how this seat bestowed great power and responsibility. His father and grandfather had ruled from this chair and now it was his. As if pulled by an unseen force, he slowly walked up the steps and stood before the chair. Dunen felt mixed feelings as he stared at the seat, remembering his father, who sat on this chair for many years while he and his brother grew up beside him; now it was he who must continue the solemn role. He then gently sat down and looked at his friends. They all watched him with pride. It comforted Dunen that he was not alone, and good friends were near to help. He then realized his mother had arrived in the hall and was also watching. She smiled with great pride. He also noticed the huge stone statues of his grandfather Anandun and the mighty general Teranda. Both had been great leaders and men of valour. Their grim stares reminded him of the immense responsibility now placed on his shoulders. Dunen felt weak, but he gathered courage as he turned his gaze back to the people who now surrounded him.

"From the dreadful events that have come to pass in these last days, and by the will of God, I now take the throne of my father and will continue his great reign. To his honour and, above all, for our God, the Lord of Hosts who has given us life and the victory today, I do take this charge, and my life is given for it."

"Long live the king!" shouted Menfre, and soon the hall rang with shouts of praise to God and in honour of the new king.

Chapter 14
THE QUEEN OF TERANDA

Months passed quickly for the city of Teranda. Dunen and Menfre had much to do after reclaiming the throne. Dunen commissioned Menfre to restore the royal guard. Men were recruited and trained to increase the depleted army. The city gates were put back in place. Spies were sent to gather news and watch carefully King Ernum's every move. So long as Ernum lived, Dunen was well aware that war with Dernak was not far away. Dunen knew that Ernum would not give up his plans to get the sword of Teranda.

Dunen also reconstructed the wall that barricaded the mountain pass of Perethes and placed guards there day and night. The pass was the least difficult path to Teranda, and Dunen knew that Ernum would use it.

As the days passed, Elena began to remind Dunen that as sole heir to the throne, it was wise of him to marry and have children to carry on the lineage and give hope to the people. Dunen agreed, and yet it troubled him much, for he knew many noble princesses, but his heart loved none of them. A royal celebration was planned at the palace for Teranda's victory and to announce the beginning of the King's courtship. As the day of the celebration approached, Dunen prayed earnestly to God for wisdom, seeking His guidance, knowing well that God would help him with his choice.

On that great day of joyful celebration in Teranda, Dunen waited alone in a parlor not far from the throne hall. As he sat on a couch, Dunen nervously rubbed his hands, as he thought upon his great decision. He was dressed in his kingly apparel of burgundy, with golden edges on his collar and sleeves. A golden lion, the emblem of his family, was stitched on his breast.

His thoughts about choosing Aristinne were often disturbed by the images of Marani. He found it difficult to forget the village girl, whom he had found interesting and beautiful. His mother would never allow his interest to fall on a tribal woman for many good reasons, and his heart was saddened at the thought.

Footsteps approached the room, and the doors opened. His mother, dressed in a light pink gown, strolled in. A great pearl necklace hung around her gentle neck. Her hair was gathered atop her head, and a golden crown, studded with diamonds, lay on it. Her beauty touched Dunen's heart with great admiration, and he rose to his feet and went to her.

"You look ever so beautiful, Mother!" Dunen said with adoration.

"Thank you. And you so handsome, my son," she complimented proudly, reaching out to hold him. "I know many women will be broken-hearted today."

Dunen blushed for a moment, but his smile faded away as the thought of his predicament returned.

"What is it, Dunen?" She asked.

"What is it? Must I tell you my heart? It is a difficult moment for me."

"Why? What troubles you?" his mother asked with concern.

"I-I am not sure."

"Have faith, my son. All will go well."

"Yes, of course," he quickly replied not wanting her to be worried.

Dunen turned away from her and breathed deeply. Calming himself, he asked God for strength. Dunen then realised he should simply leave the situation in God's hands. Straightening his posture, he turned to his mother.

"I am nervous, but I will what is required. Let us

go. Our friends wait for us."

Although disturbed by his attitude, Elena decided not to delve deeper. Dunen offered her his arm and both left the room.

In the throne hall, musicians filled the room with a joyous sound, as noblemen and ladies, dressed in their lavish apparel, waited for King Dunen's entrance. Menfre, Danar and Manru were mingling with the guests.

Two loud knocks on the floor by the doorkeeper attracted everyone's attention, and their voices were hushed. The musicians, at the same time, silenced their instruments. The great hall doors opened and Dunen entered the room, leading his mother. Without looking to either side, the two walked across the hall to the throne. The gentlemen and ladies bowed respectfully as the royal pair passed by. Dunen placed himself before the throne as his mother stood parallel to his right. All remained silent as Dunen looked over the guests, and as they waited for his welcome.

"It is our honour to welcome you here today. My mother and I wish you great joy. We have much for which to thank our Lord God, for the peace that reigns in Teranda, which by His grace will endure.

The Lord bless you and let us enjoy this great time together," he concluded and then took his seat.

The guests returned to their conversations as the musicians began their joyful music once again. Many questioned if tonight Dunen would choose his bride, and who it would be. This was the moment Dunen dreaded. The ladies who sought him for marriage would present themselves before him during the evening. The one to whom Elena would give her consent with the customary nod, Dunen would then take by the hand and invite her to sit beside him for a time. This would demonstrate to all his interest in courtship and most likely marriage.

As he sat, guests and friends came before him, bowing and thanking him for the invitation. Some he knew well, and relatives to the family members spoke of their joy in seeing him and of other matters, this being the first time in many days that they had time together. Some ladies of the city presented themselves, only to be welcomed by Dunen with a short bow, none of which Queen Elena had given her consent.

Finally, Aristinne presented herself before Dunen. Dunen was glad to see her and could sense the expectation of his guests as they waited breathlessly because many knew of their close friendship.

"Hello, Aristinne."

"Good evening, my lord. I thank you for your kind invitation to this great house and its friends," she said as she bowed before him.

She was a beautiful lady and of strong character. Dunen had shared many joyful moments with her when they were young, and he had much respect for her family.

Hesitantly, Dunen turned to his mother to receive the expected consent, but found to his great astonishment that she abstained. Dunen was confused as well as embarrassed before Aristinne. Confirming her decision, Elena made it clear that she did not consent, but only offered a smile.

"You are most welcome Aristinne and we thank you for your presence," Elena said.

Aristinne also felt confused and hid her great disappointment.

"Thank you, my lady. It is my great joy to see you and an honour to be invited," she said as calmly as possible.

Dunen did not know what to say. "Well, ah...I hope you enjoy yourself," he blurted out.

Aristinne bowed quickly and withdrew herself.

Dunen was still stunned by his mother's reaction and embarrassed for Aristinne as she gave him a last bewildered look.

"Mother! What have you done?" he asked in a whisper, while hiding his reaction from the guests. Noticing she did not answer his question, but was staring with great interest out into the hall, he looked to see what caught her attention. Another lady approached the throne. At first, he could not discern who she was, and felt worried he had forgotten some other noble lady. As she drew closer his heart almost stopped at the moment he recognised Marani. Delicately she came forward to the steps of the throne and bowed.

She was dressed like the other princesses, her dark auburn hair tied back and set on her head. Pearls were on her ears and around her neck, contrasting against her dark skin. Her light pink dress accentuated the warm color of her skin. Dunen could not believe how beautiful she looked.

"My heart rejoices to see you again, King Dunen, and I am honoured to have been invited," she said with a controlled smile. She turned to Elena and bowed again. "I am most honoured to see you again, my lady."

"I am glad to see you as well, Marani," Elena said

happily.

Dunen was wide-eyed with bewilderment over their casual and familiar greeting, and looked at his mother for some explanation. She returned his gaze and nodded her consent.

Marani's surprise visit almost made him forget why his mother nodded. As he remembered, joy and peace flooded within him so strongly that he froze for a moment, overwhelmed by the emotions. He then returned his attention to Marani. Her smile drew him to his feet. Entranced by her eyes, he reached out for her hand and it was rewarded to him.

"Would you sit by my side?" Dunen could barely say.

"Yes, my lord," she answered as calmly as she could. Her face radiated the great joy and love she had within.

Her voice stirred a great happiness within him. He guided her up the steps of the dais and to the chair beside the throne. All the guests were silent with surprise and with great curiosity concerning the identity of the unknown lady.

Dunen could not take his eyes from hers as he looked on great joy. All of a sudden, a great shout was heard in the hall.

"Long live the king!" someone bellowed, and all looked to see a grinning Bilob, dressed in the best possible city clothes that could fit him. Beside him stood Mandara his mother and Celkob, both overjoyed of the joining. Bilob shouted again, and soon all joined him in a great chorus, as they honoured the king, his mother, and the future queen of Teranda.

This first book ends with the rise of Dunen, second son of Favro, to the throne of Teranda. Yet much still must be told of his perilous journey to the dark regions of Sousenden, and of the strange people of Daouk. During this time, Ernum's desire for the sword of Teranda grows ever greater after failing to possess it. His hand stretches even farther from his domain as he tries to conquer all who oppose him and achieve his ultimate plan.

A legendary sword, hidden but not forgotten, brings war to the royal family of Teranda. Personal and spiritual revelations shake the family's core as they face not only their failures but an ever-growing menace. Dunen, the youngest son of King Favro, is forced to take on the inevitable task of righting his family's wrongs and save his kingdom.

www.swordsofmenandangels.com

ISBN 978-0-359-64989-1
90000

9 780359 649891